IN 2016, I DECIDED TO SPEND THE YEAR SENDING OUT SHORT MINICOMICS TO A SMALL GROUP OF FRIENDS AND FANS. I WAS THINKING A LOT ABOUT THE IDEA OF COMICS AS GIFT GIVING; THE GIFT OF SHARING YOURSELF WITH A READER, THE GIFT (AND THRILL!) OF AN UNEXPECTED COMIC SHOWING UP IN YOUR MAILBOX. I WAS STRUGGLING WITH AN INTEREST IN ANONYMITY, A DESIRE I OFTEN STILL HAVE TODAY TO HIDE BEHIND MY WORK; MANY OF THESE COMICS WERE ORIGINALLY UNSIGNED OR JUST SIGNED AW. I LIKED THE IDEA THAT THE COMICS WOULD SHOW UP UNANNOUNCED, WITH NO CONTEXT. IT FELT FUN, AND A LITTLE DUMB, AND A LITTLE MYSTERIOUS. MANY PEOPLE SENT BACK KIND NOTES OR THEIR OWN COMICS. I FELT A LACK OF PRESSURE THAT ALLOWED ME TO TRY NEW THINGS.

THIS BOOK COLLECTS MOST OF THOSE 2016 COMICS, WITH SOME LIGHT EDITS, AS WELL AS FIVE NEW STORIES THAT ATTEMPT TO RECAPTURE AND BUILD ON THE MOOD OF THE 2016 WORK. REREADING THAT WORK NOW, I SEE A DESIRE TO BECOME A BETTER WRITER AND A SEARCH FOR NEW WAYS OF MAKING MARKS. I REMEMBER I COMMITTED TO DRAWING SIMPLY, ALMOST ENTIRELY IN PENCIL. I NOTICE THAT MANY OF THESE STORIES ARE AMONG MY MOST AUTOBIOGRAPHICAL, THOUGH OTHERS ARE STRAIGHT FICTION.

I ALSO NOTICE THAT MY DESIRE TO BE MYSTERIOUS SEEPS INTO THE STORIES — MAYBE AT THE EXPENSE OF CLARITY, IN A FEW CASES. BUT THIS ALSO CREATES A MOOD OF INTIMACY THAT I HOPE RECREATES, EVEN IN THIS COLLECTION, THE FEELING OF REACHING INTO YOUR MAILBOX AND PULLING OUT A FLIMSY, TINY COMIC. A WHISPERED SECRET. A SCRIBBLED MEMORY.

THANK YOU, ALWAYS, FOR READING.

—ANDREW WHITE

DECEMBER 2020

# CONTENTS

you look out into
the darkness
and you know

you are alive

ONE.
you walk out
on to
the balcony
your friends are
sitting inside, talking
right through that
sliding glass door
their voices intermingle
pleasantly with the
buzzing stillness

below you

a city
at night

shimmers
through layers
of blackness

(close your eyes
and hear the
wind whistle)

fingers
drumming

you let the
minutes turn
inward on
themselves

you're somehow
sucked towards
the darkness
laid out in front
of you

close your
eyes

the quietness
rushes by
your ears

This image often flits around the edges of my mind, as I race down the highway in the early hours that shouldn't count as morning.

A solitary figure, barely visible through the thick night.

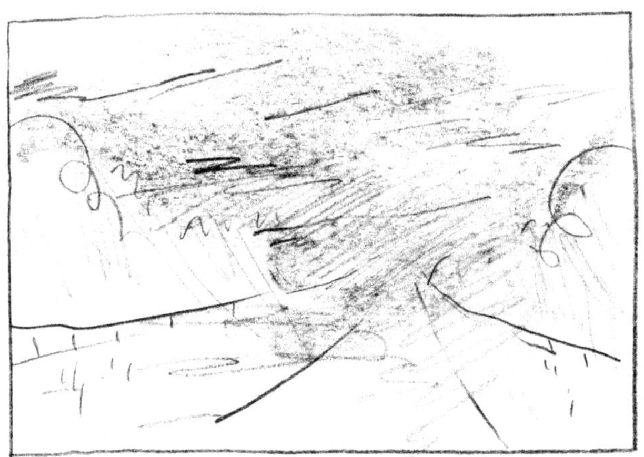

i glance
over

and there
it is

silently watching

# THREE.

hi
yeah
you're just
breaking up a
little

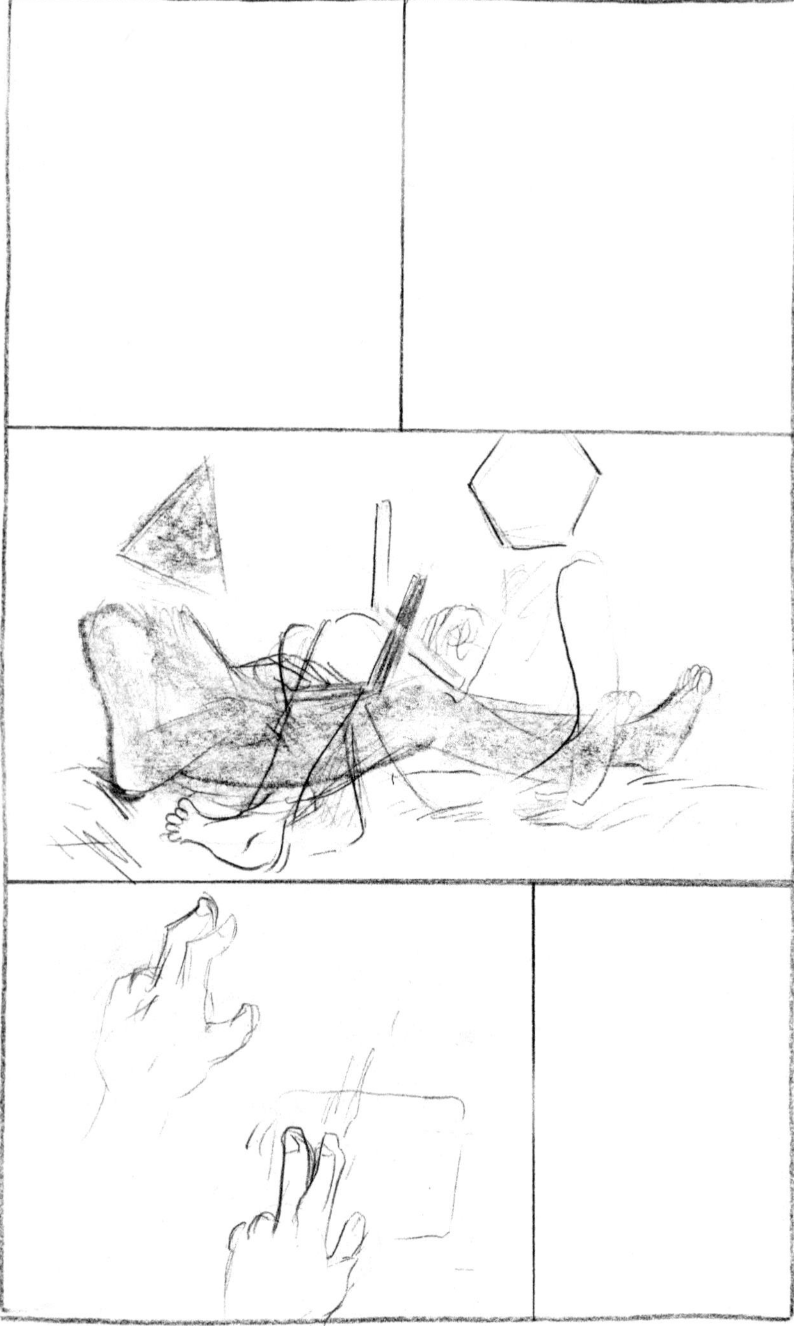

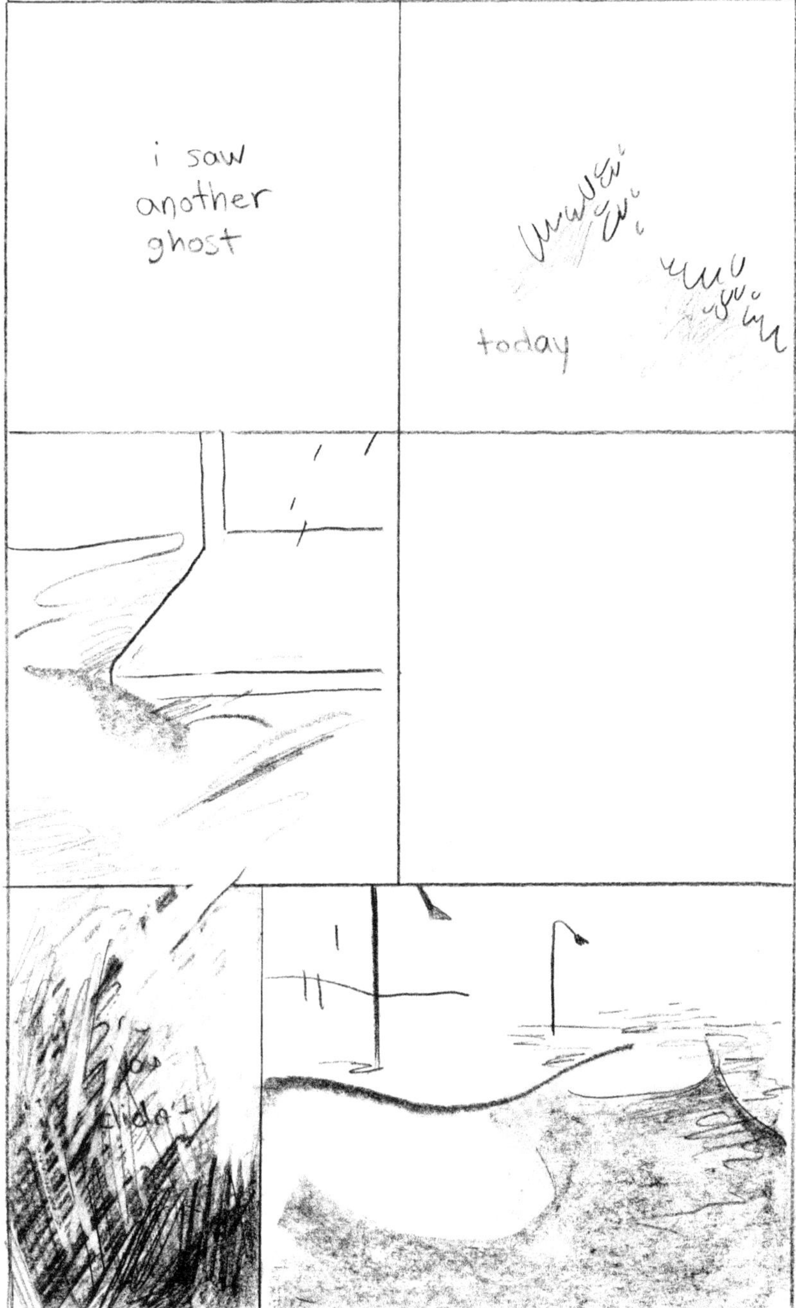

i saw
another
ghost

today

tell me
what
happened

okay

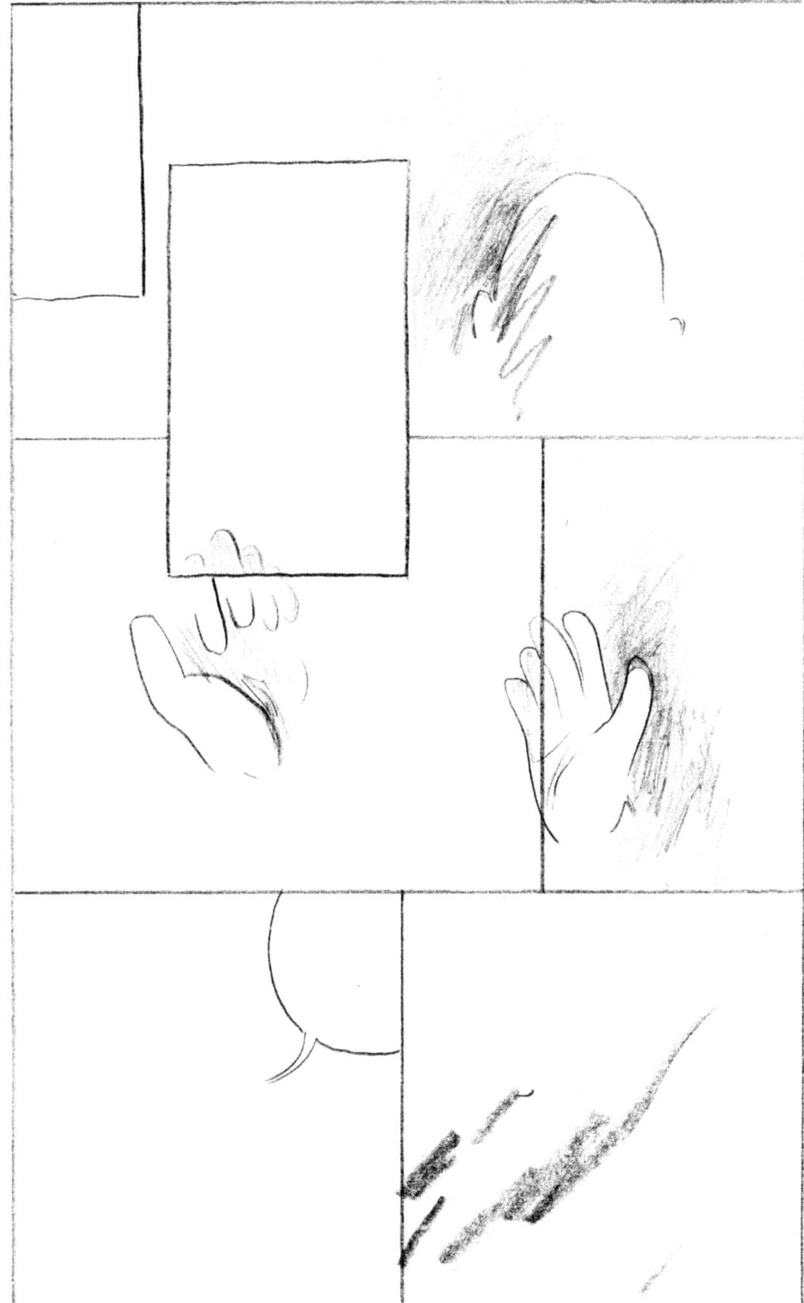

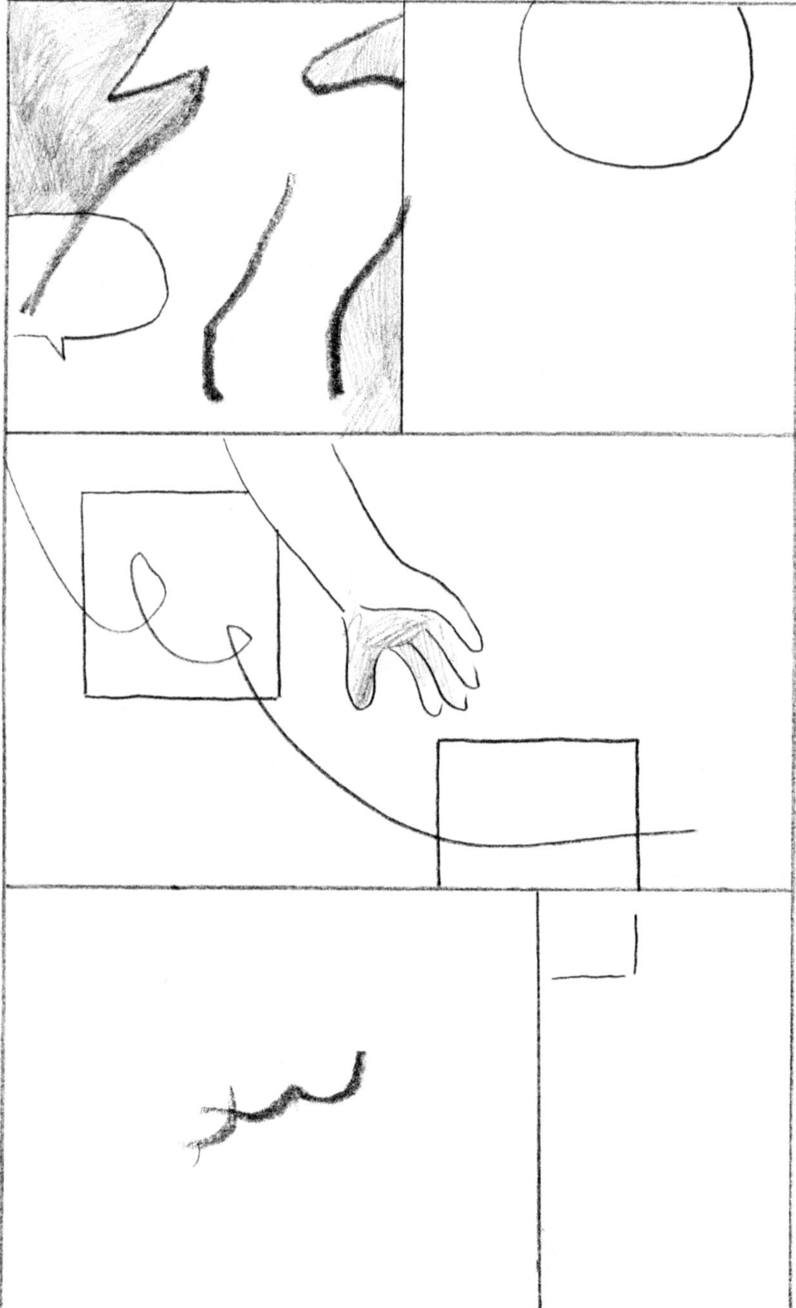

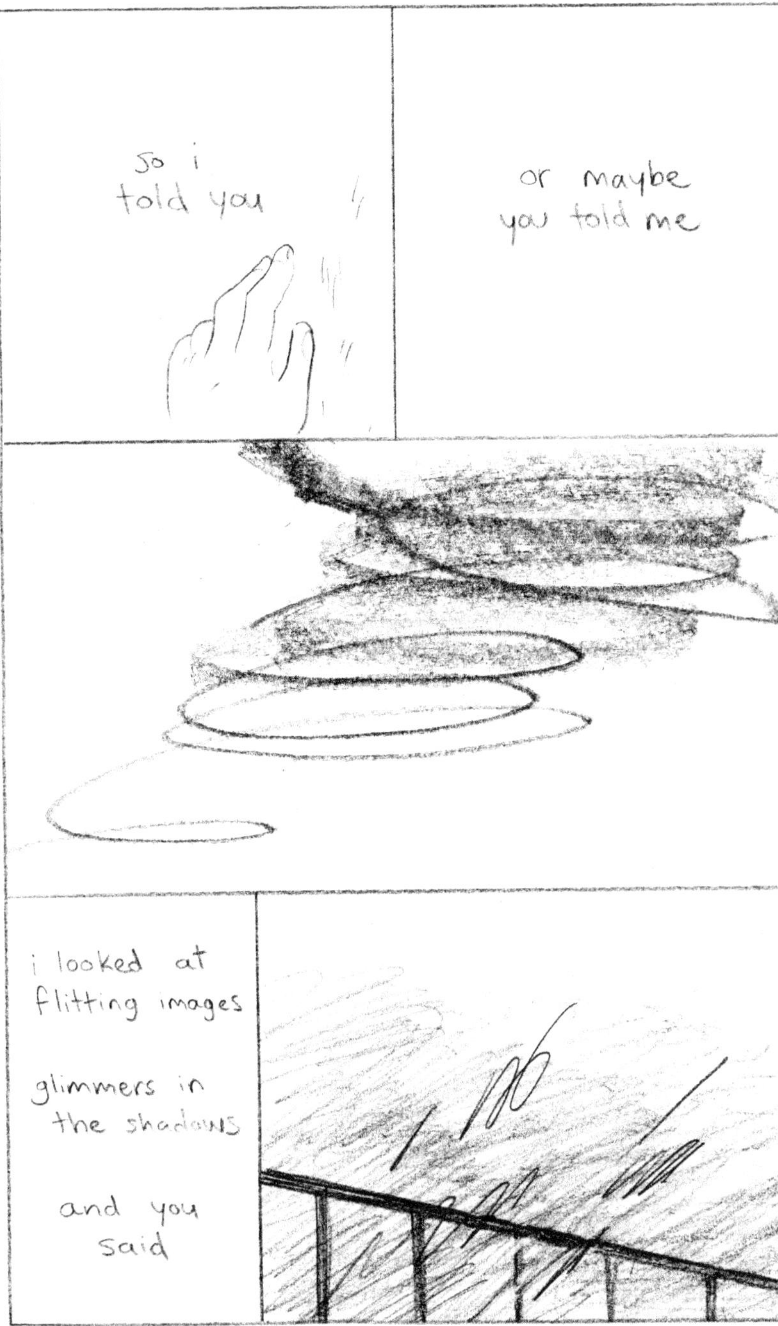
so i
told you

or maybe
you told me

i looked at
flitting images

glimmers in
the shadows

and you
said

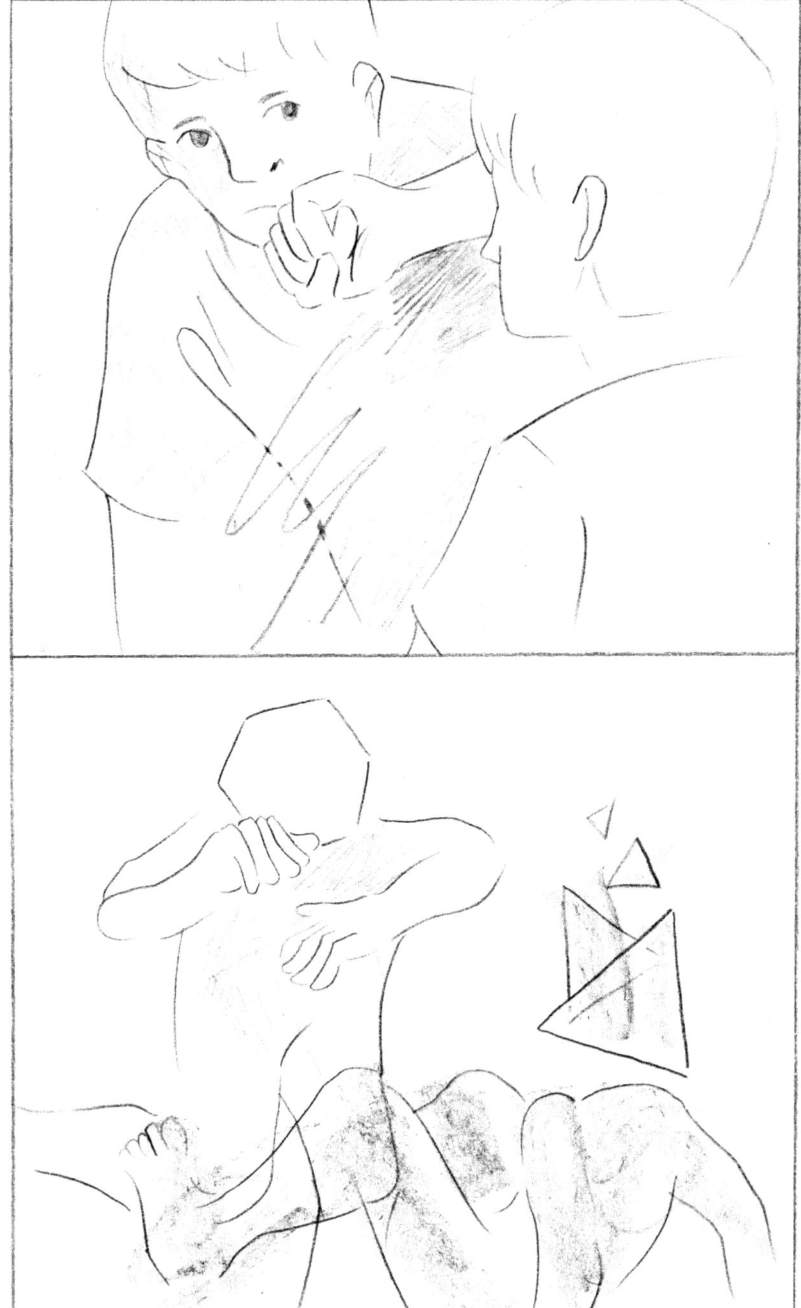

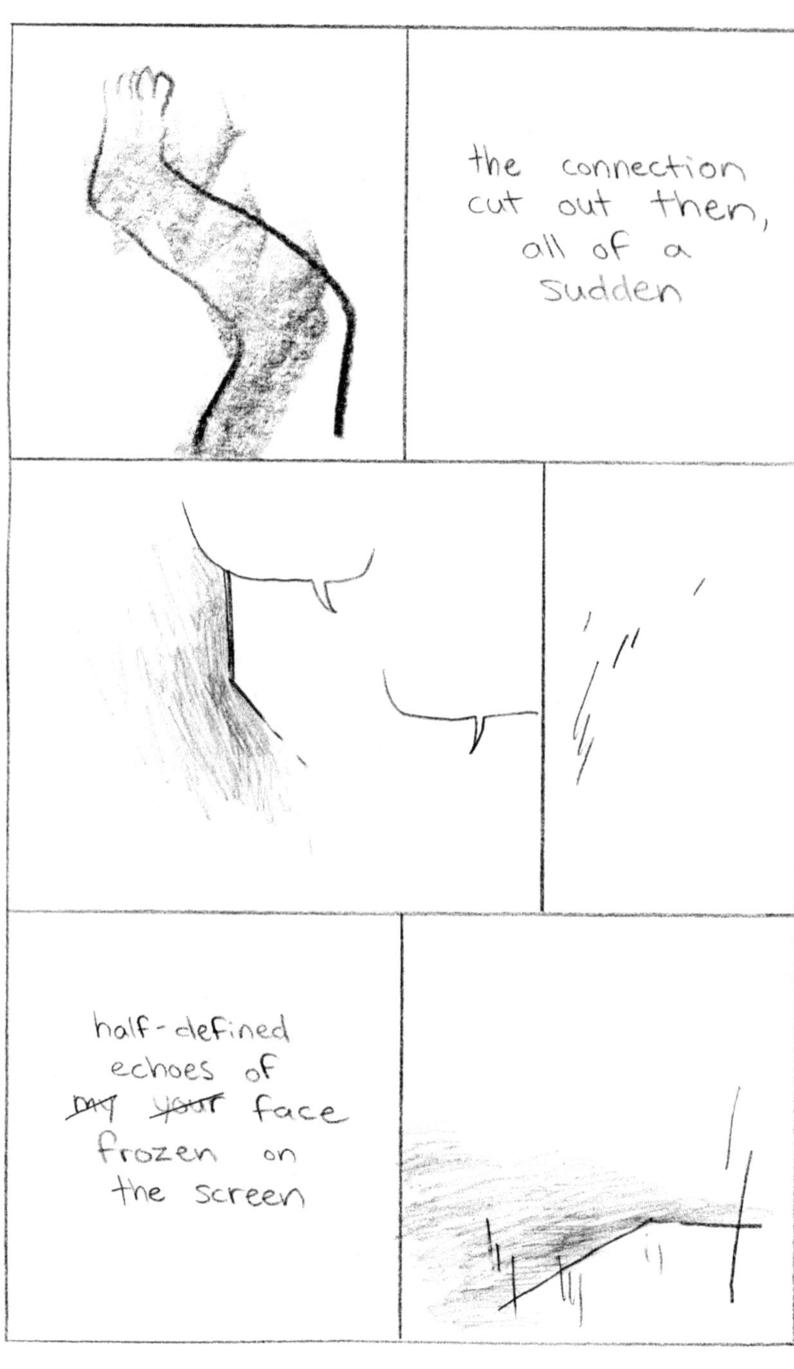

the connection
cut out then,
all of a
sudden

half-defined
echoes of
~~my your~~ face
frozen on
the screen

i tried to call you back

but for some reason i couldn't
get through

so instead i thought about
what you had said.

FOUR.

you told me
once about
walking back
out to that
balcony in
the dead
of the night

you said you
were surprised
because the
tenor and hum
of the silence
had changed
completely

you kept talking and i kept listening. or i tried to, at least.

but i also listened to the sound of your voice. it went something like

no, that's not right. it's more like this:

no, it's softer.

but also sharp. rigid.

keep talking. i need to listen just a little more carefully and then i'll be sure

THE YEAR THAT
SHE WENT MISSING

ONE EVENING, LINDA'S SISTER CALLED.

IT WAS LIKE A HIDDEN SWITCH HAD BEEN FLIPPED, AND SUDDENLY THEY WERE BOTH SCREAMING. IT FELT AWFUL. EVEN IF THEY HAD VERY MUCH WANTED TO, LINDA AND HER SISTER HAD NEVER YELLED AT EACH OTHER BEFORE.

LINDA THREW UP TWICE. ONCE IN THE AIRPORT AND
ONCE ON THE PLANE. BOTH TIMES SHE SECRETLY
HOPED SOMEONE WOULD SEE HER AND SAY SOMETHING
SO SHE LINGERED, HER BREATH RAGGED, A LITTLE
LONGER THAN SHE HAD TO.


ESPECIALLY ON THE PLANE, SHE WAS SURPRISED
THAT ONE OF THE FLIGHT ATTENDANTS DIDN'T
ASK IF SHE WAS ALRIGHT. THERE WAS A GROUP
OF THEM STANDING RIGHT OUTSIDE THE
BATHROOM. THEY MUST HAVE HEARD.

THE REST OF THE FLIGHT WAS UNEVENTFUL. LINDA FELT LIGHTHEADED, SO SHE DRANK A LOT OF WATER. SHE HAD A SHORT CONVERSATION WITH HER SISTER THAT LEFT THEM BOTH FRUSTRATED AND SAD. THEY SAT ON THE PLANE IN SILENCE AND LINDA HAD TO REMIND HERSELF WHY THEY WERE TAKING THIS TRIP.

THE PLANE LANDED. WEEKS PASSED.

AS LINDA AND HER SISTER TALKED, THE SINK WAS
DRIPPING. OUTSIDE, THE COOL WIND AND THE
NIGHT AIR AND THE WAVERING STREETLIGHTS ALL
SWIRLED TOGETHER.

LINDA AND HER SISTER KEPT TALKING, EVEN
AFTER THEY HAD RUN OUT OF THINGS TO SAY.

EACH MORNING, LINDA TALKED TO HER SON AS SHE SAT CURLED IN A BALL ON THE CORNER OF THE BED. SUDDENLY, A YEAR HAD PASSED AND HER CONVERSATIONS WITH HER SON WERE ONLY WEEKLY. BUT SHE STILL ROSE EARLY EACH MORNING, SHUFFLING THROUGH A HOUSE THAT HUMMED WITH SILENCE.

WHEN LINDA FINALLY RETURNED HOME, HER SON
ASKED LOTS OF QUESTIONS ABOUT THE TRIP.
HIS GAZE WAS PENETRATING AND STILL, AND
LINDA DID HER BEST TO COMBAT IT WITH
NON-ANSWERS.

THE TRIP WAS GOOD, SHE SAID. IT WAS NICE
TO SEE HER FAMILY AGAIN.

PAUL KNEW HIS MOTHER WAS DIFFERENT WHEN SHE CAME HOME. BUT HE WASN'T SURE WHAT HAD CHANGED, SO HE WATCHED HER VERY CAREFULLY. HE SPENT MANY YEARS TRYING TO DECIDE IF THE CHANGES WERE GOOD OR BAD.

OLD NIGHTS
FEEL LONGER

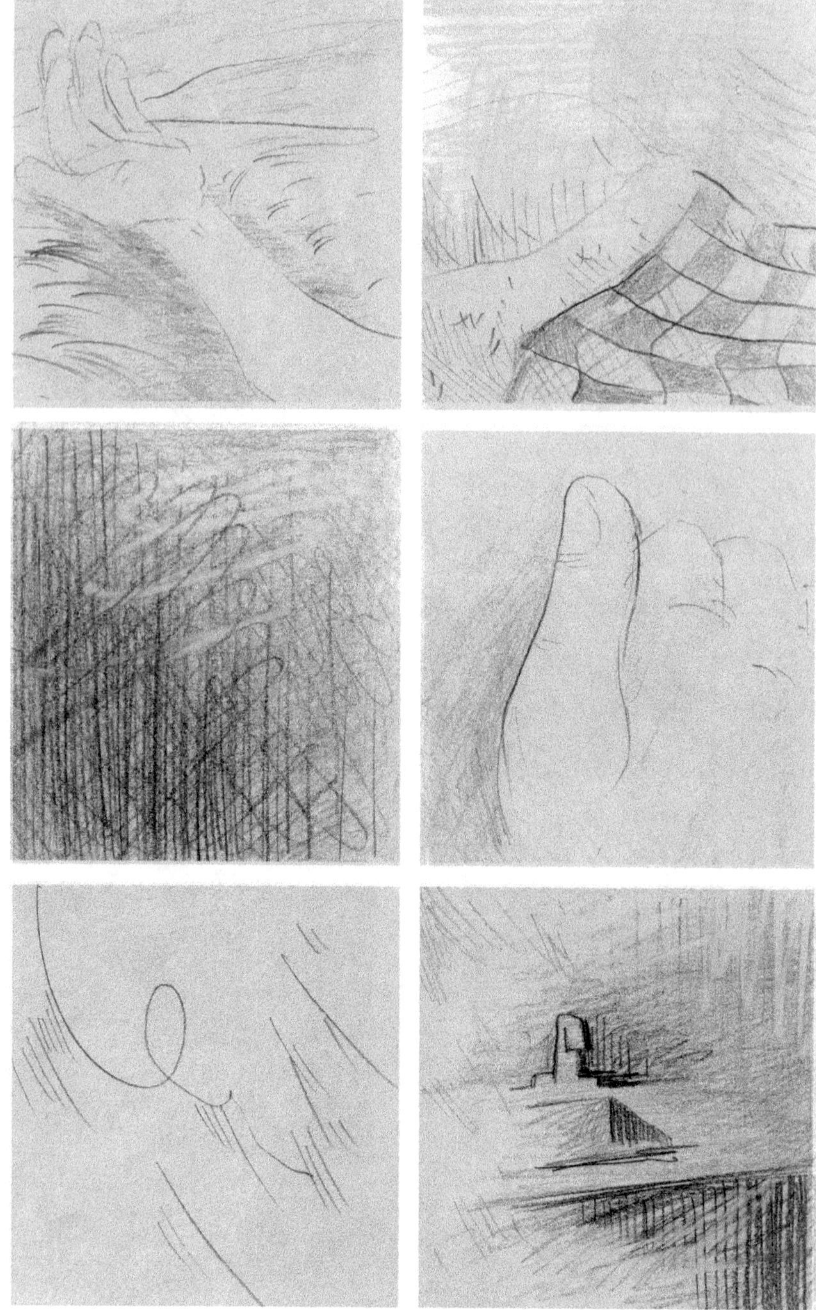

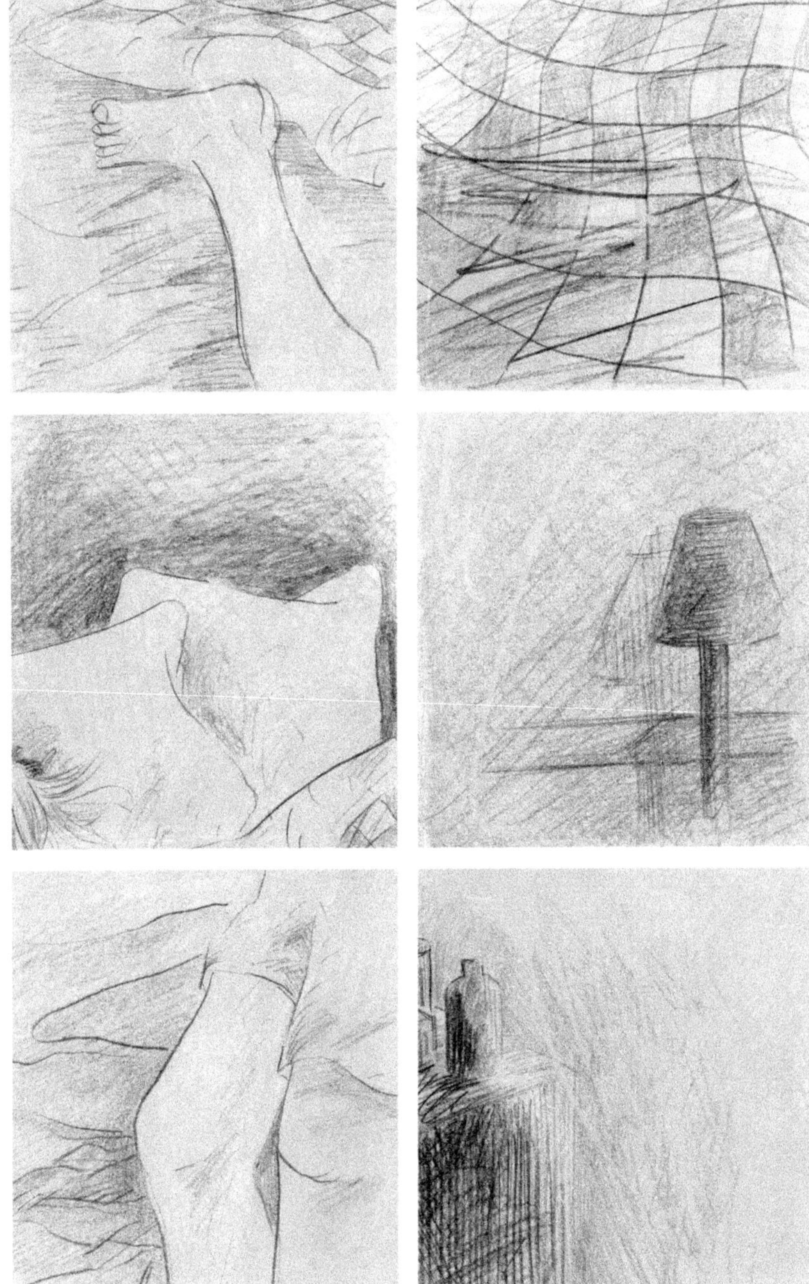

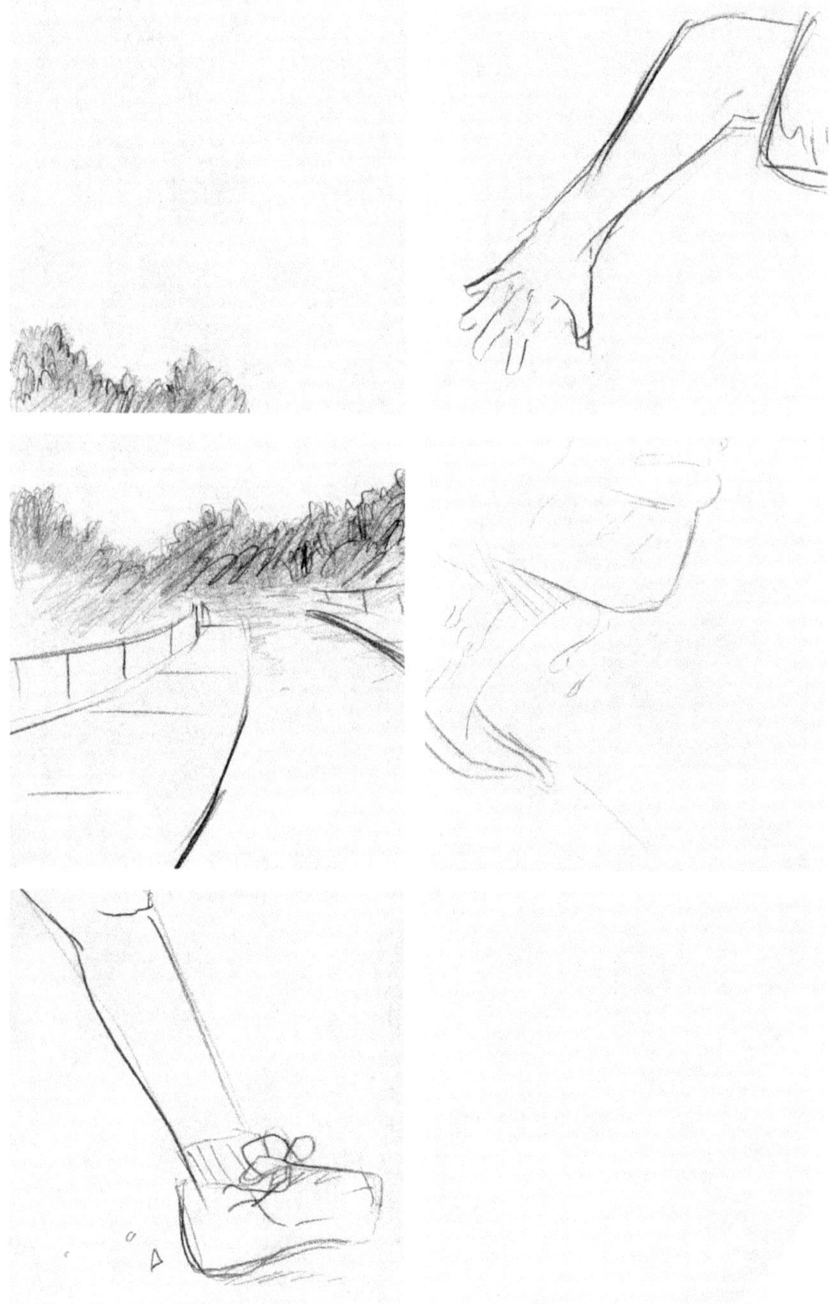

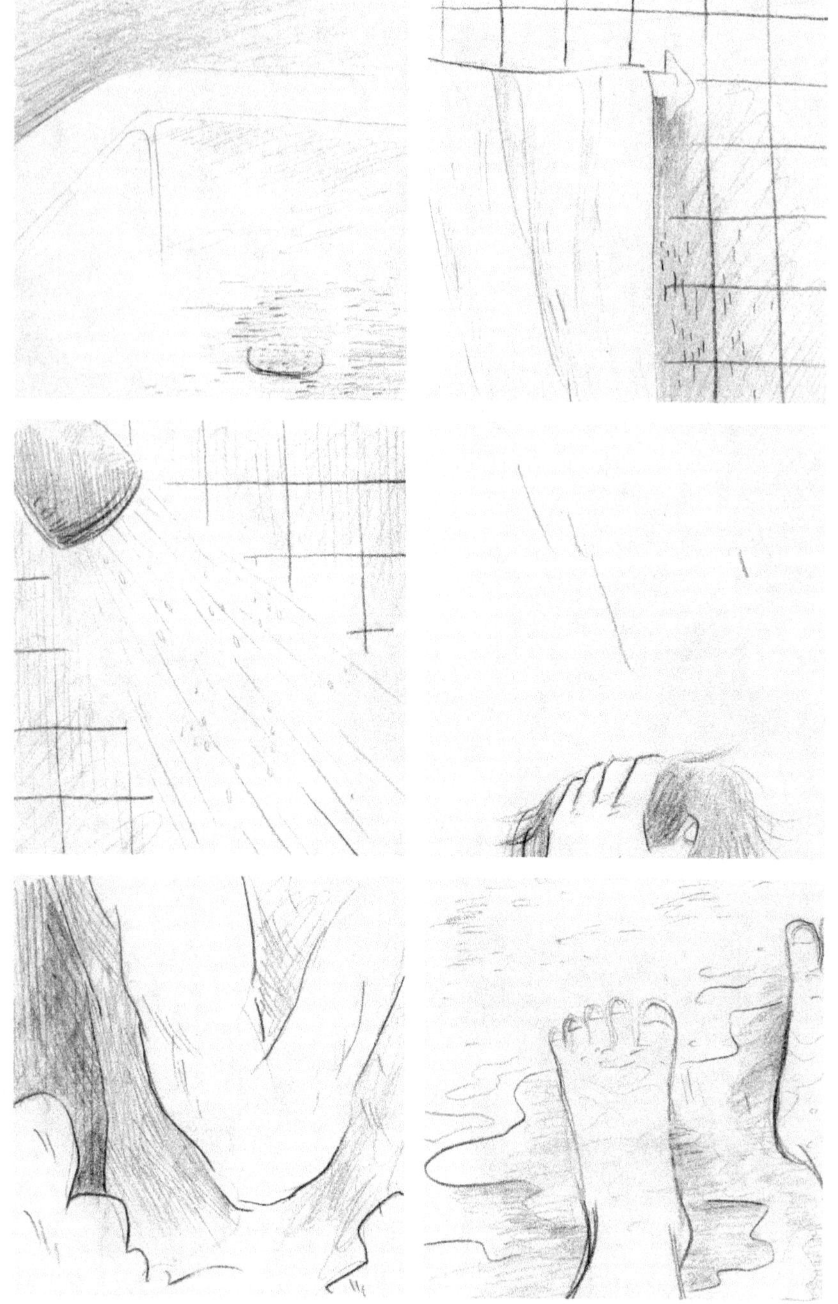

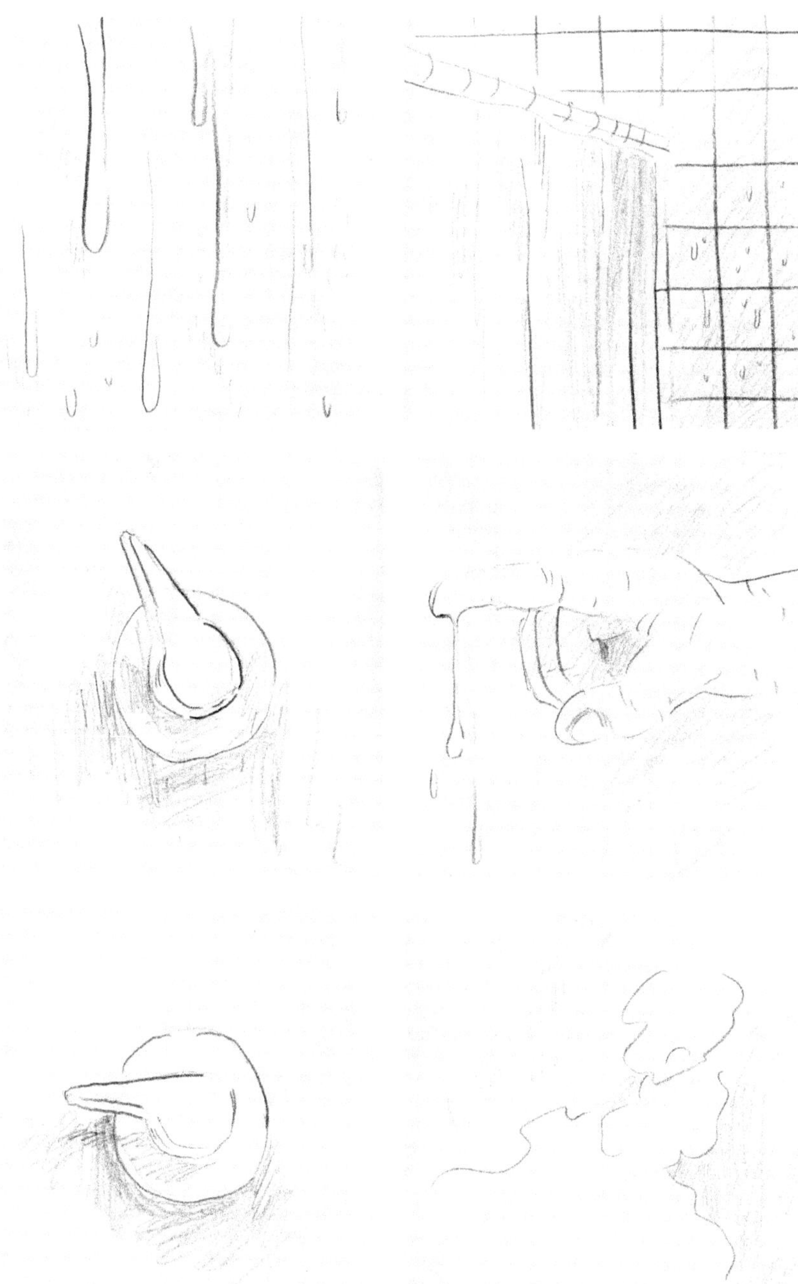

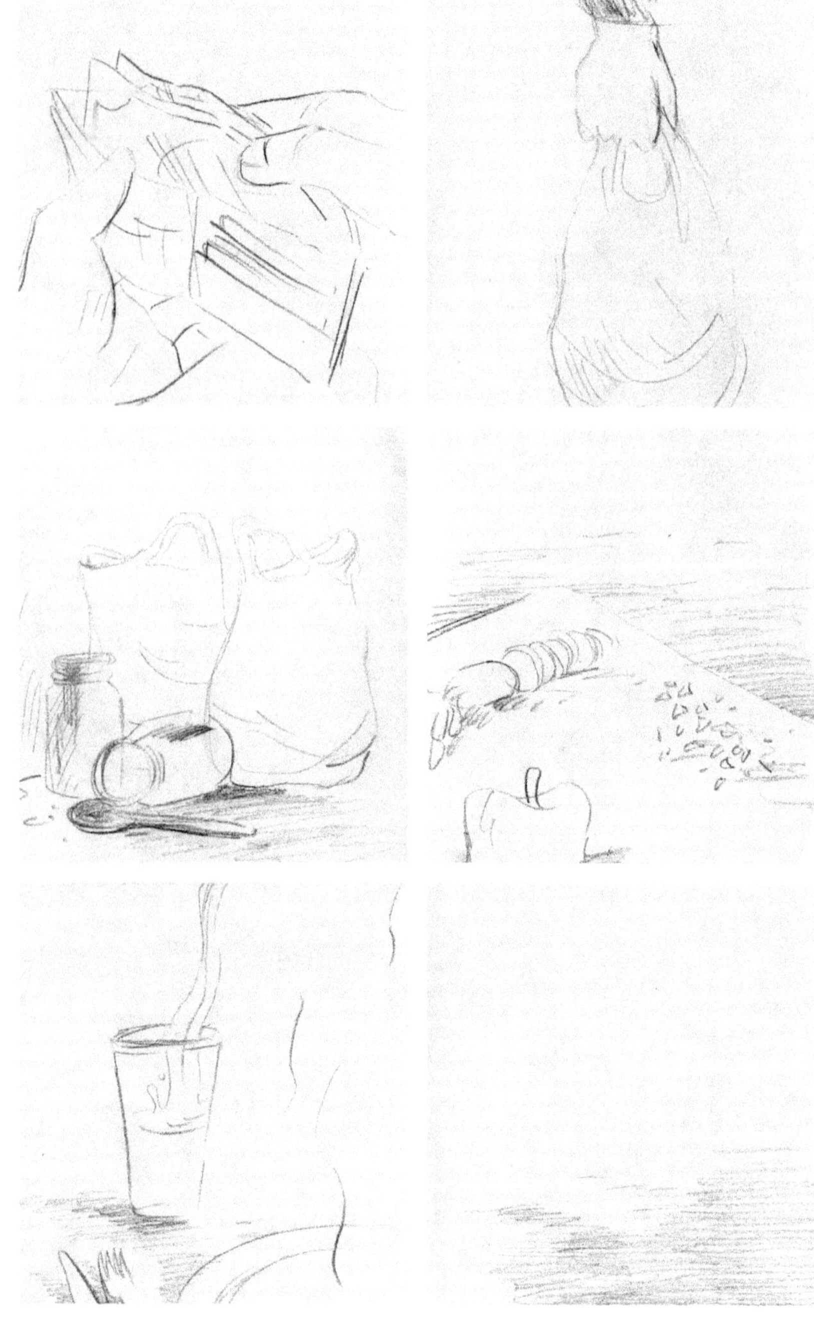

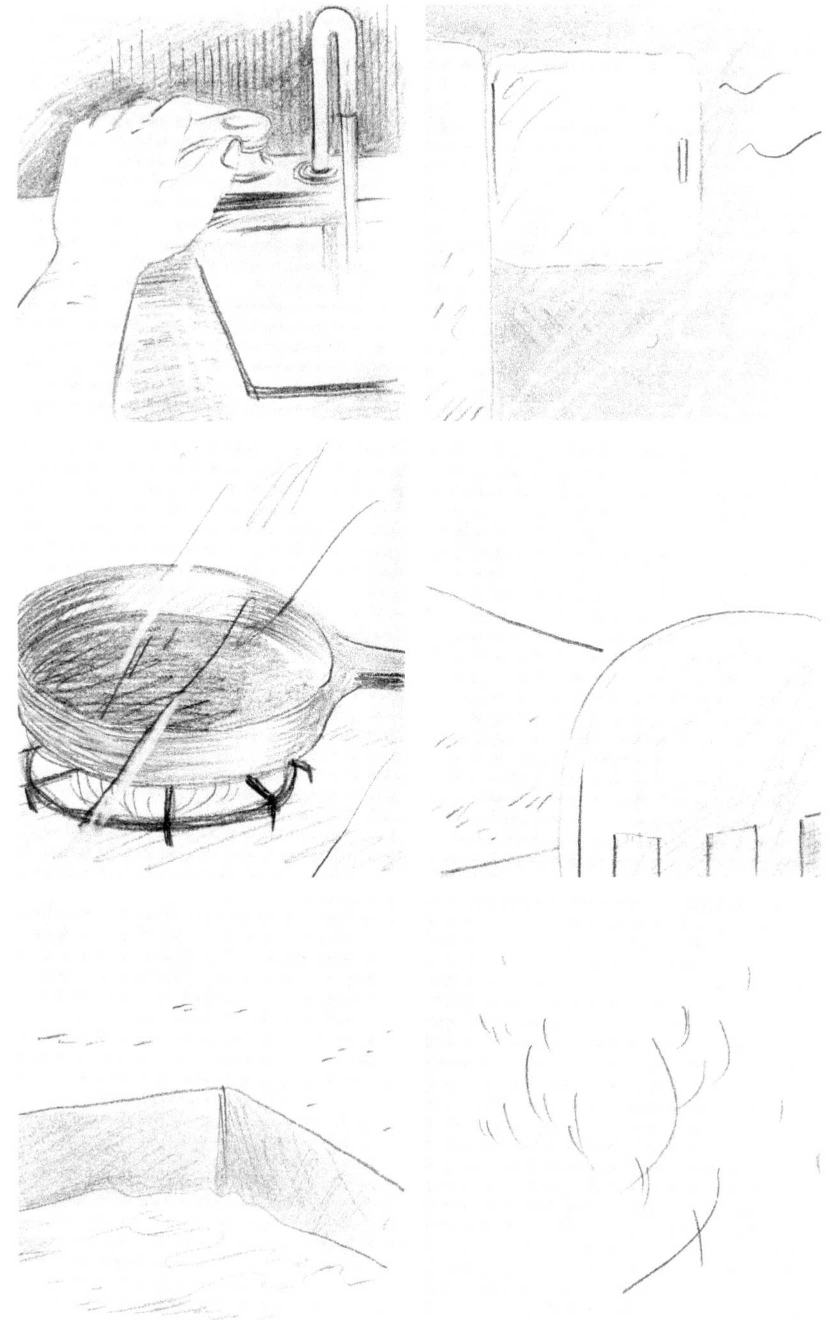

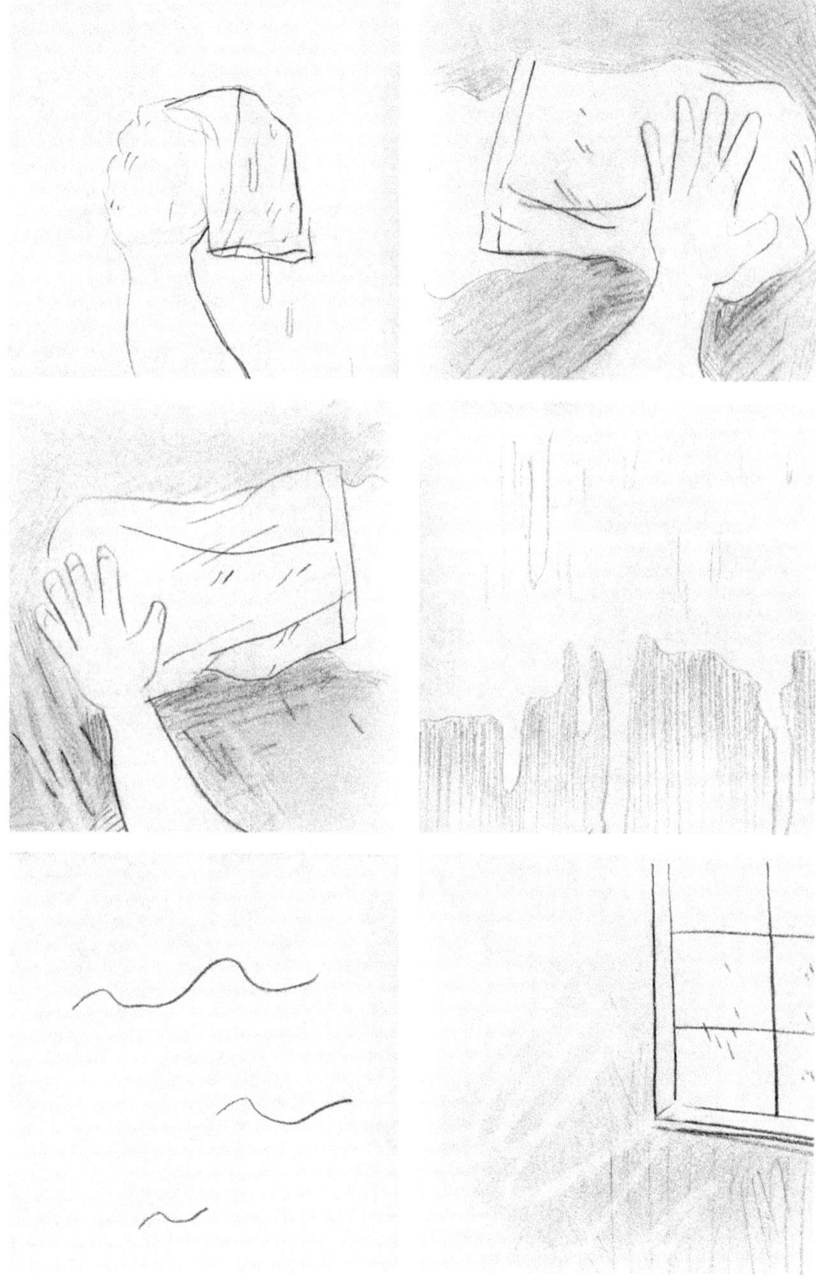

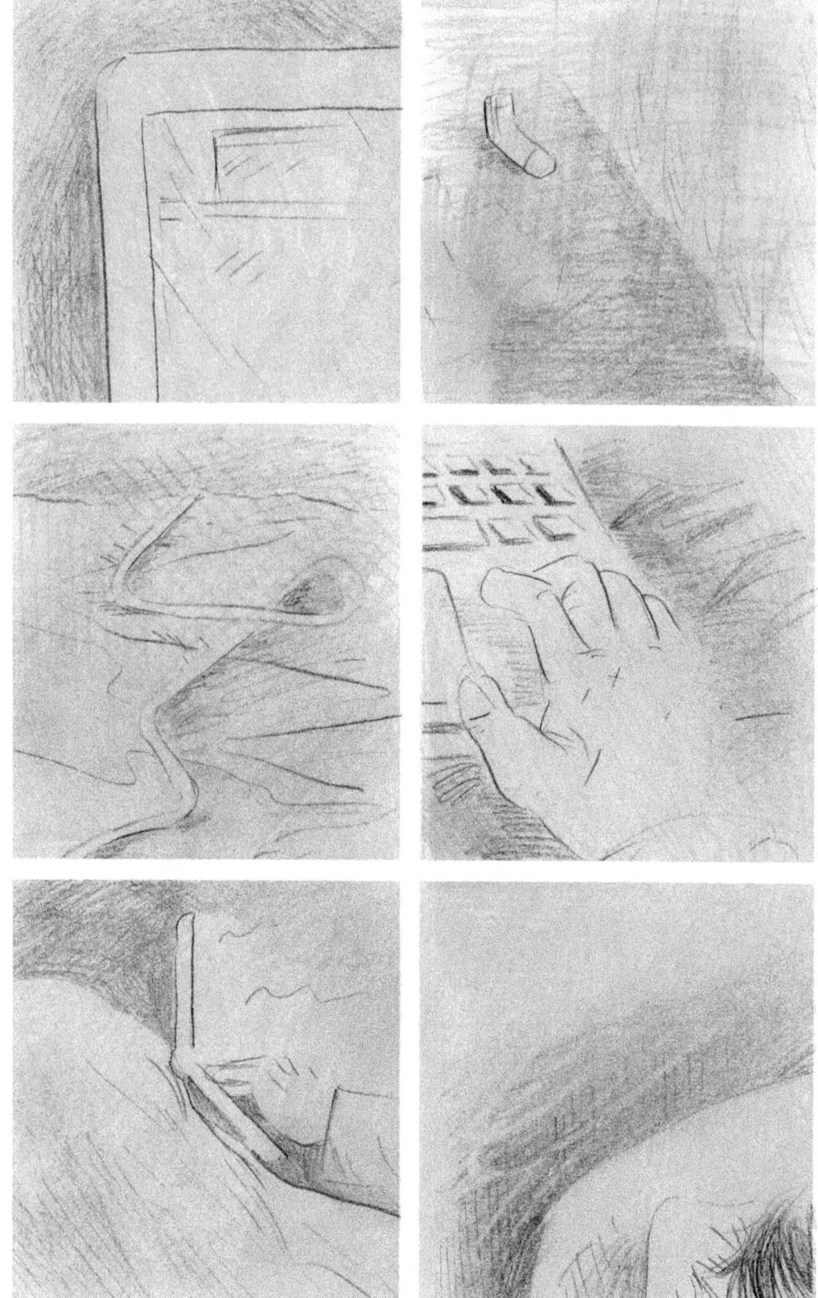

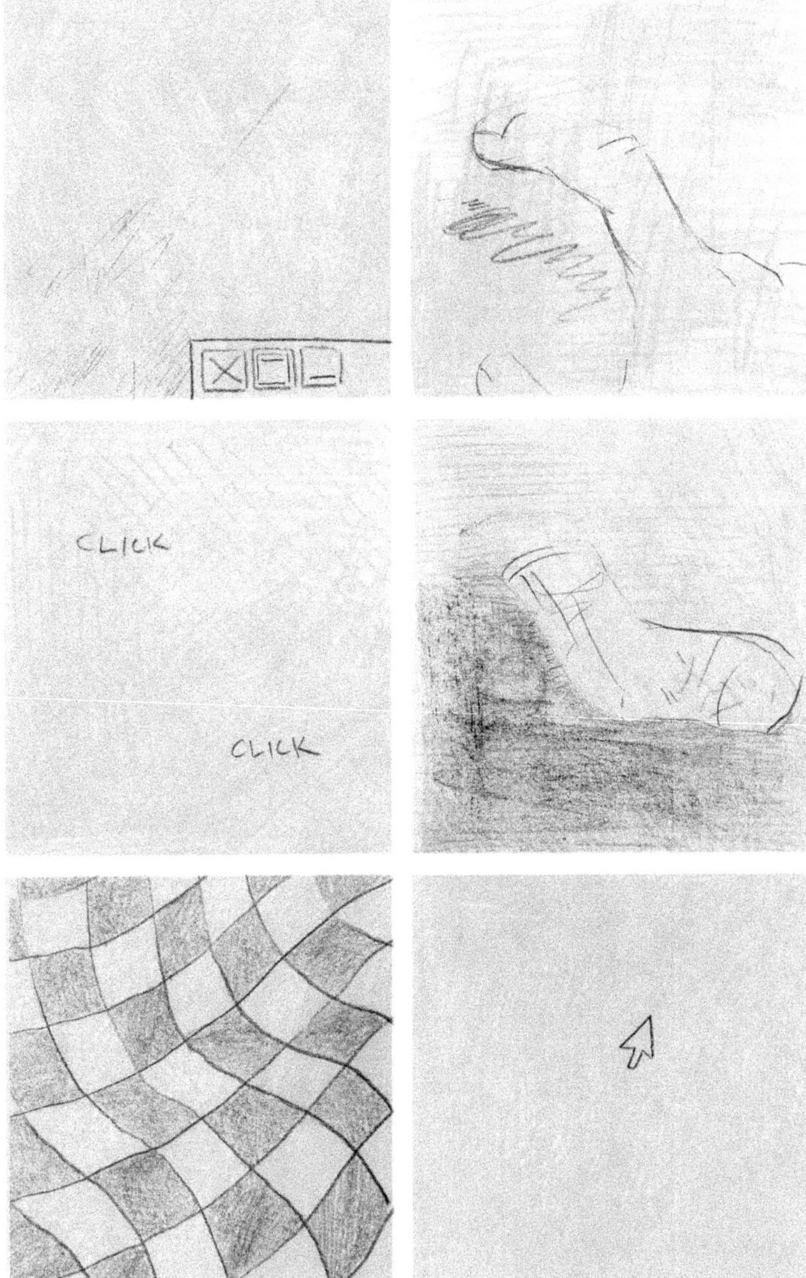
CLICK
CLICK

LETTERS I'LL
SEND TOMORROW

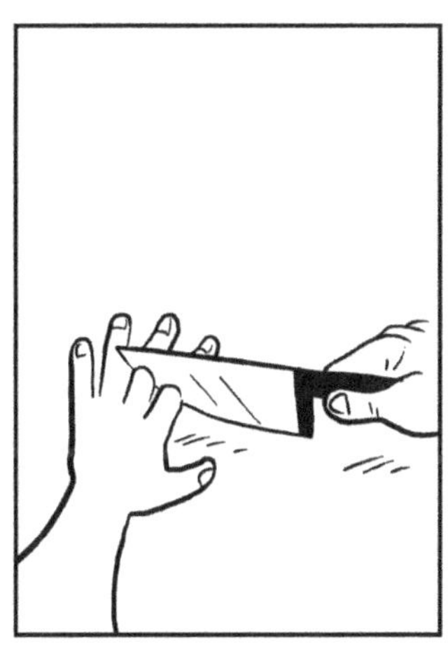

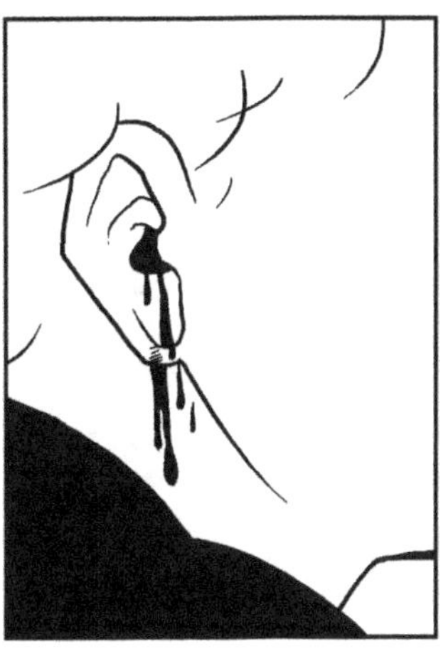

(wet)
(damp grass)

(i try to close
my eyes)

FLIP

i can't
i can't
i can't


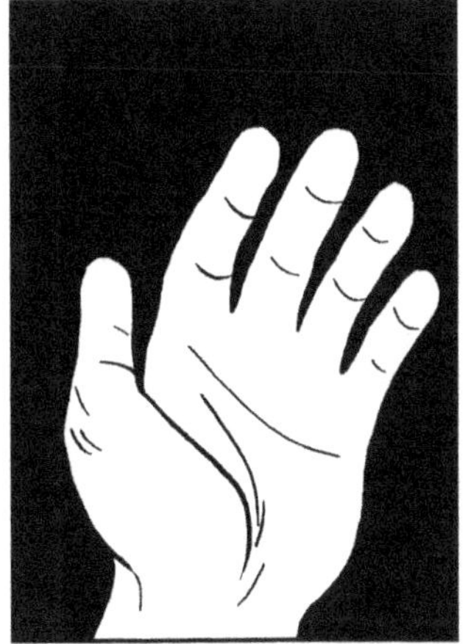

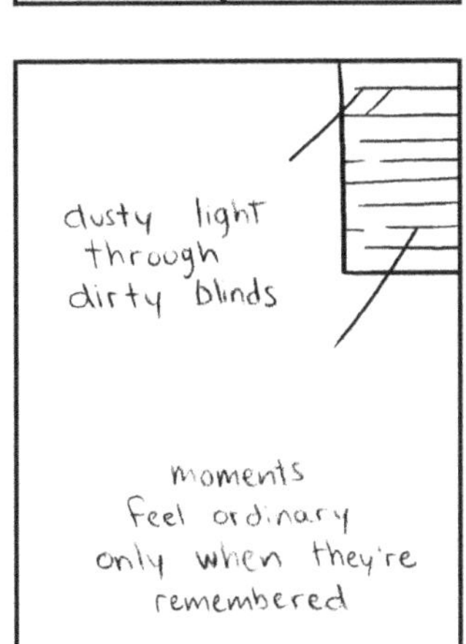

dusty light
through
dirty blinds

moments
feel ordinary
only when they're
remembered

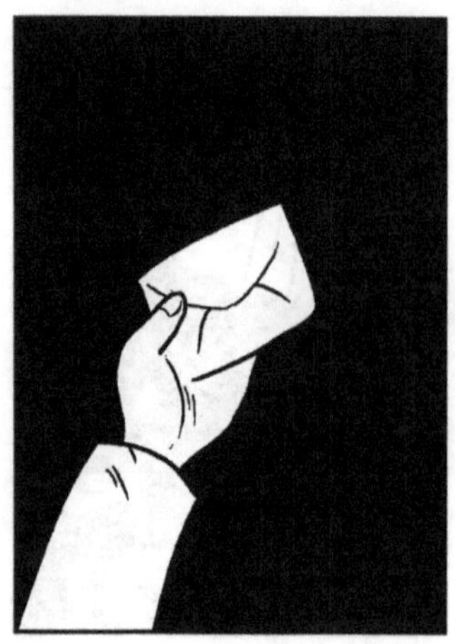

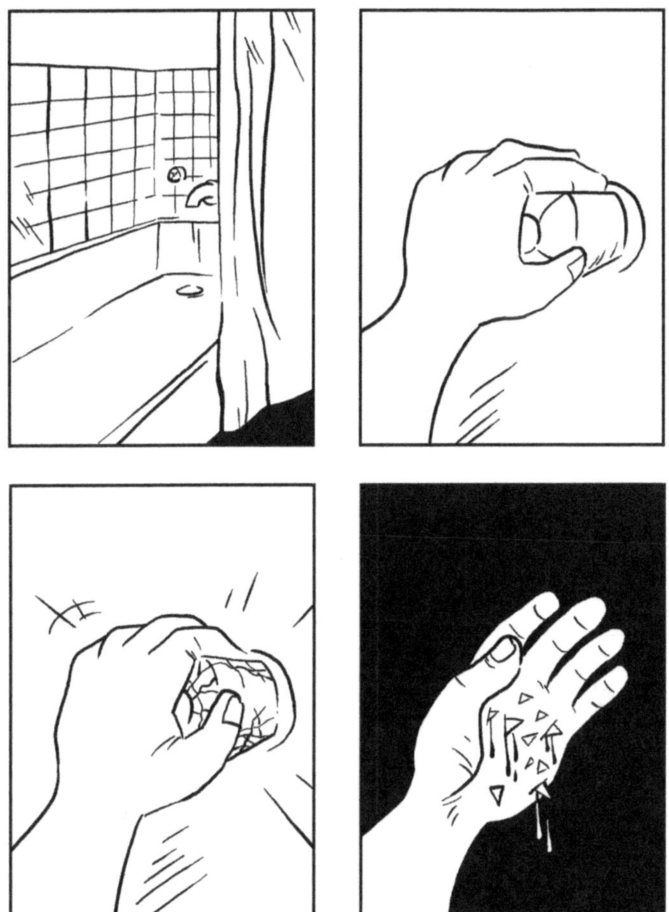

there are images that
pass me by too quickly


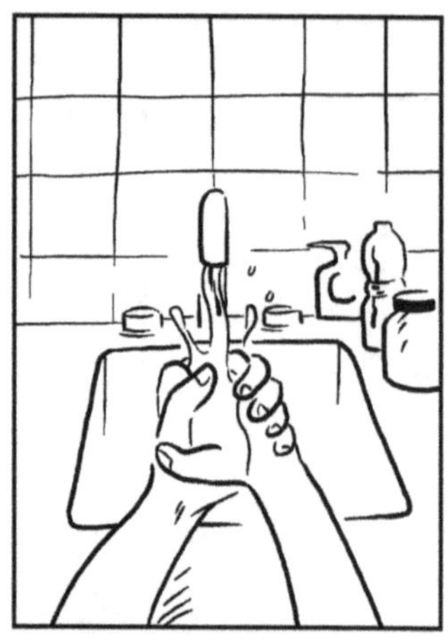

words that i repeat
like incantations

# THE  FAULTS

IN 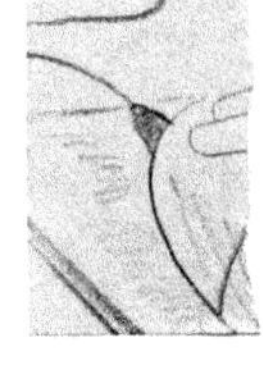

# FAULTLINES

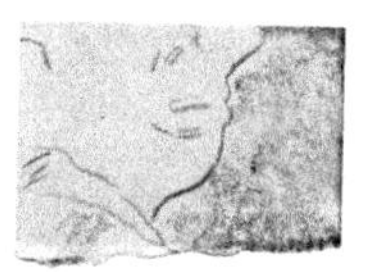

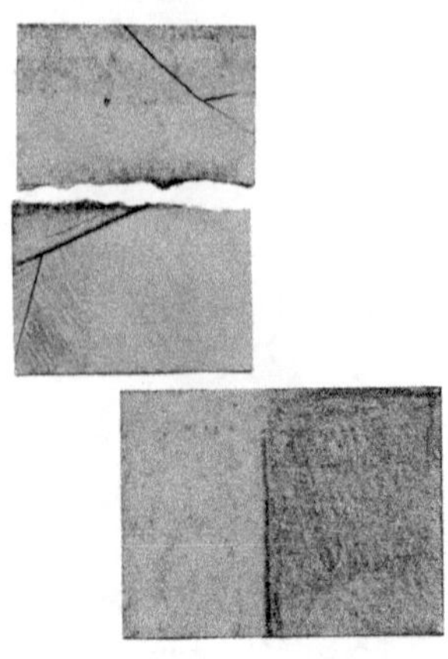

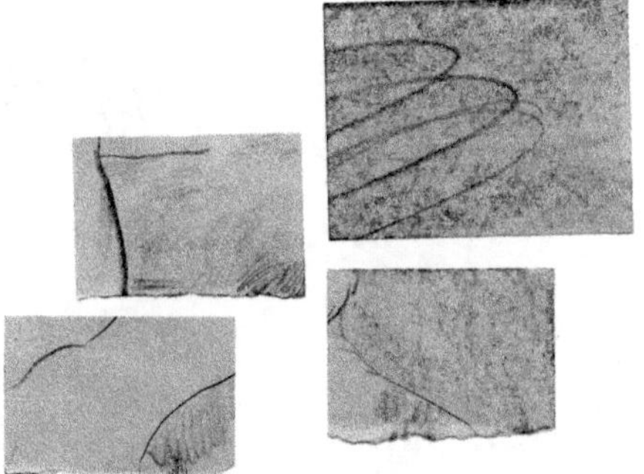

WHAT, PRAY TELL, IS THE DIFFERENCE BETWEEN THE GHOST WHOSE PASSAGE THROUGH OUR CHEST LEAVES A COLD CHILL
AND THE DREAM THAT SNAPS US AWAKE IN AN ICE COLD SWEAT

WHAT, PRAY TELL, IS THE DIFFERENCE BETWEEN
THE GHOST WHOSE PASSAGE THROUGH OUR CHEST
LEAVES A COLD CHILL AND
THE DREAM THAT SNAPS US AWAKE
IN AN ICE COLD SWEAT.

WHAT
DIFFERENCE
AWAKES
US
WHAT DREAMS
WHAT
DREAMS
PASS THROUGH
OUR CHEST
WHAT DREAMS

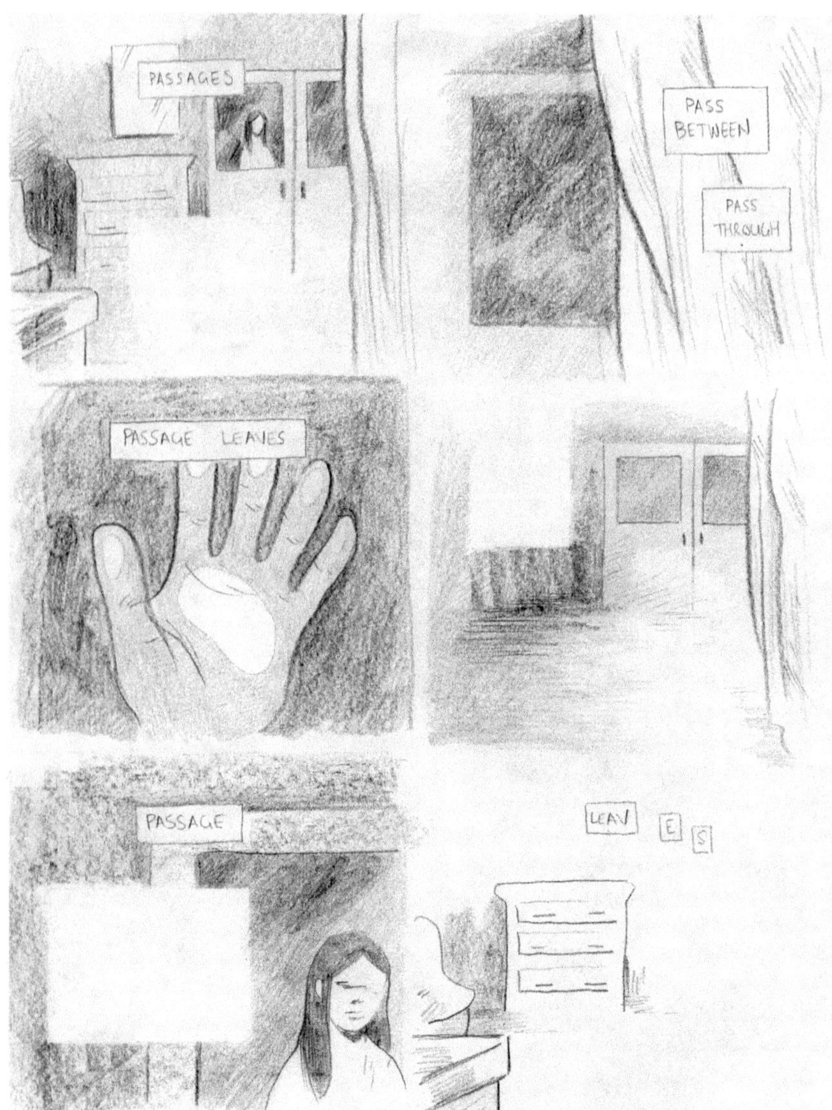

PASSAGES
PASS
BETWEEN
PASS
THROUGH
PASSAGE LEAVES
PASSAGE
LEAV E S

WHAT PASSAGE
WHOSE PASSAGE
DREAMS PRAY
PRAY DREAMS
WHAT PRAY TELL
IS THE DIFFERENCE
BETWEEN
BETWEEN
BETWEEN

TELL,
GHOSTS
T O
LEAVE
THE
COLD CHILL
L, IS T
EN          S
TELL  S
S
U
BETWEEN
WH          IS T
LE    S

AND DREAM S ?
TH IN ICE
T RA I L S
US
AND AWAKE S

it would have to be better
but it is a good thing

(written by iphone predictive text function)

I HAD
A GOOD DAY
A FEW YEARS
BACK

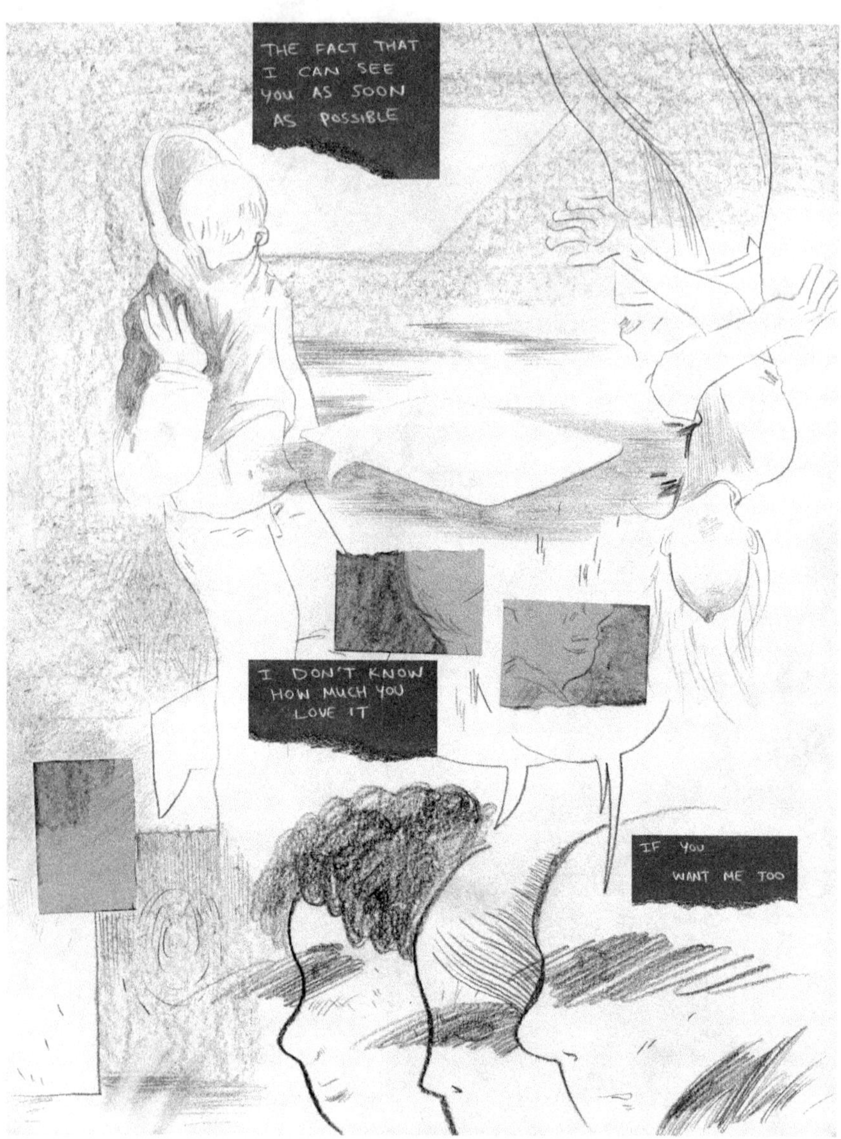

THE FACT THAT I CAN SEE YOU AS SOON AS POSSIBLE
I DON'T KNOW HOW MUCH YOU LOVE IT
IF YOU WANT ME TOO

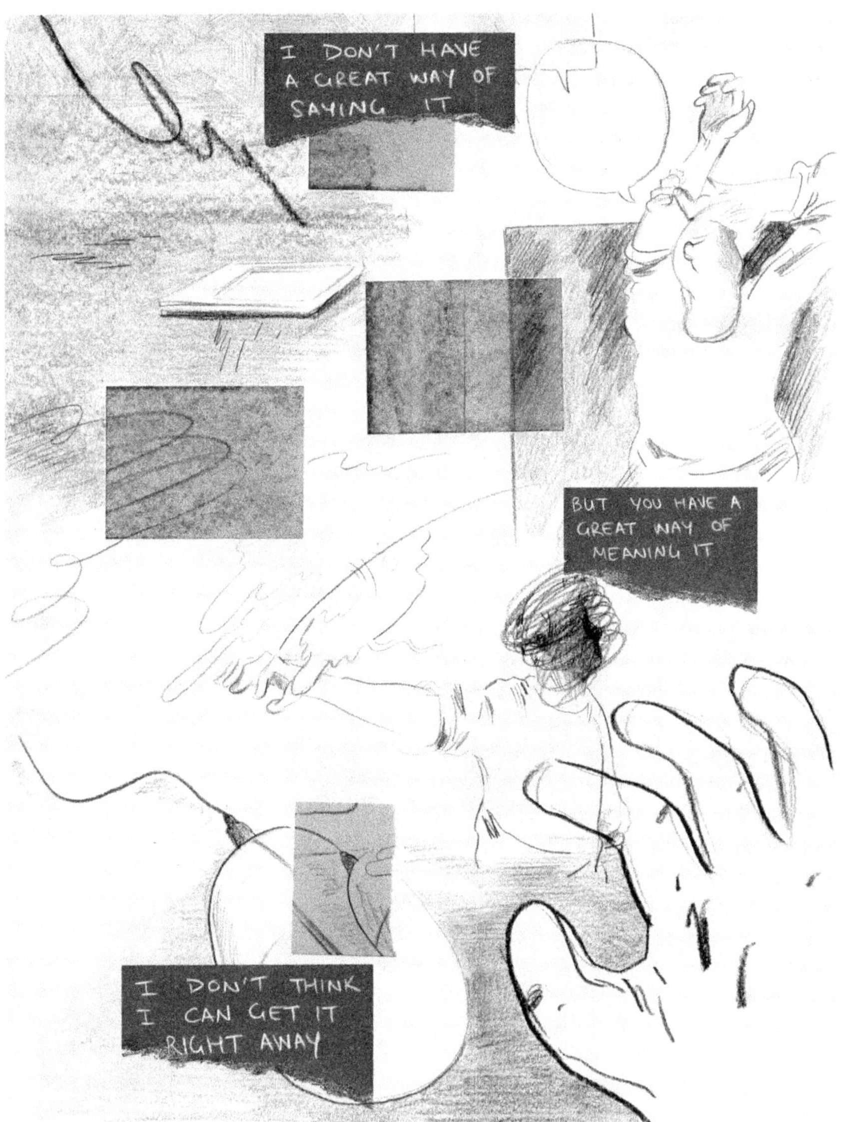

I DON'T HAVE A GREAT WAY OF SAYING IT
BUT YOU HAVE A GREAT WAY OF MEANING IT
I DON'T THINK I CAN GET IT RIGHT AWAY

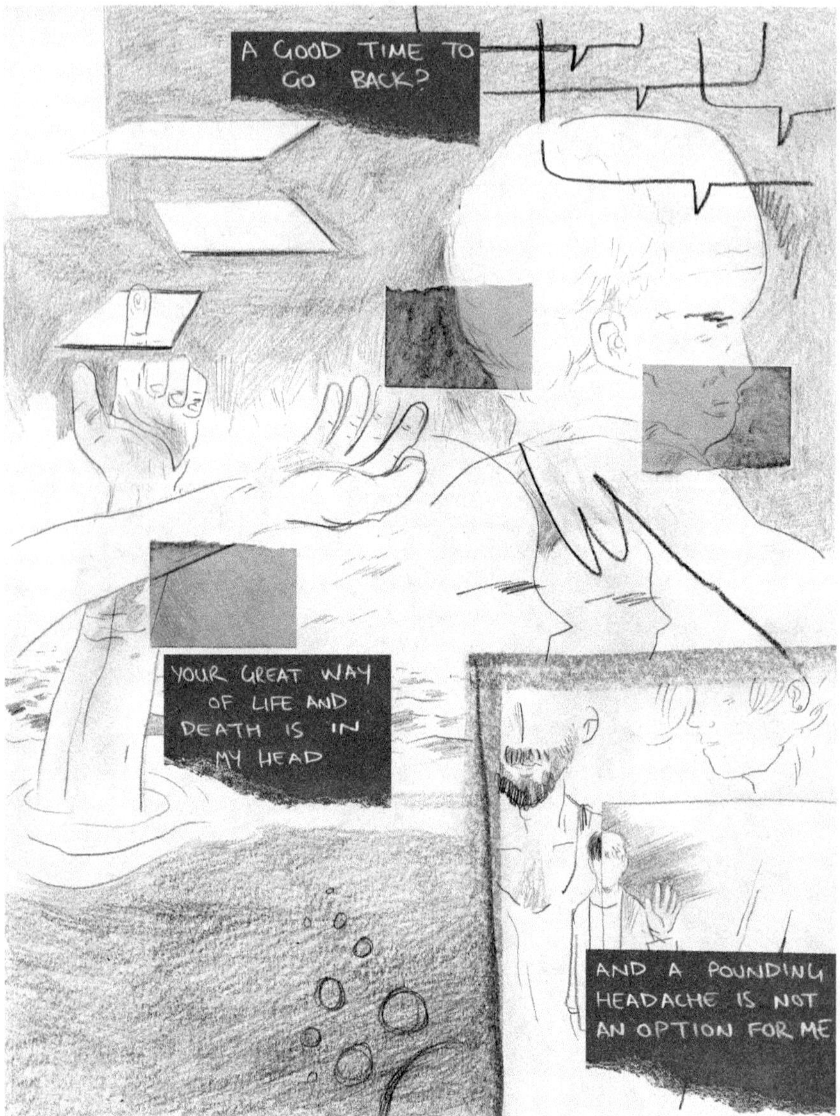

A GOOD TIME TO GO BACK?
YOUR GREAT WAY OF LIFE AND DEATH IS IN MY HEAD
AND A POUNDING HEADACHE IS NOT AN OPTION FOR ME

SAYING IT WOULD MEAN THE WORLD IS NOT THE ISSUE
I HAVE A GREAT WAY OF LIFE
SO GREAT I CAN'T EVEN SEE IT IN MY HEAD

- seeking
joy -

IT STARTED WHEN CLAUDIA SLIPPED ON A SMALL WET PATCH.

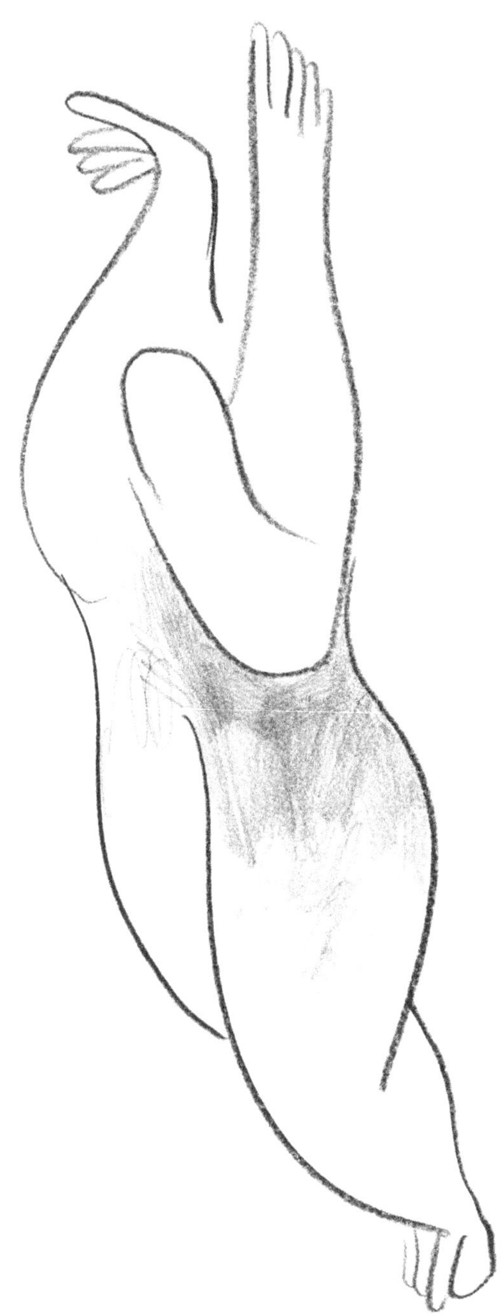

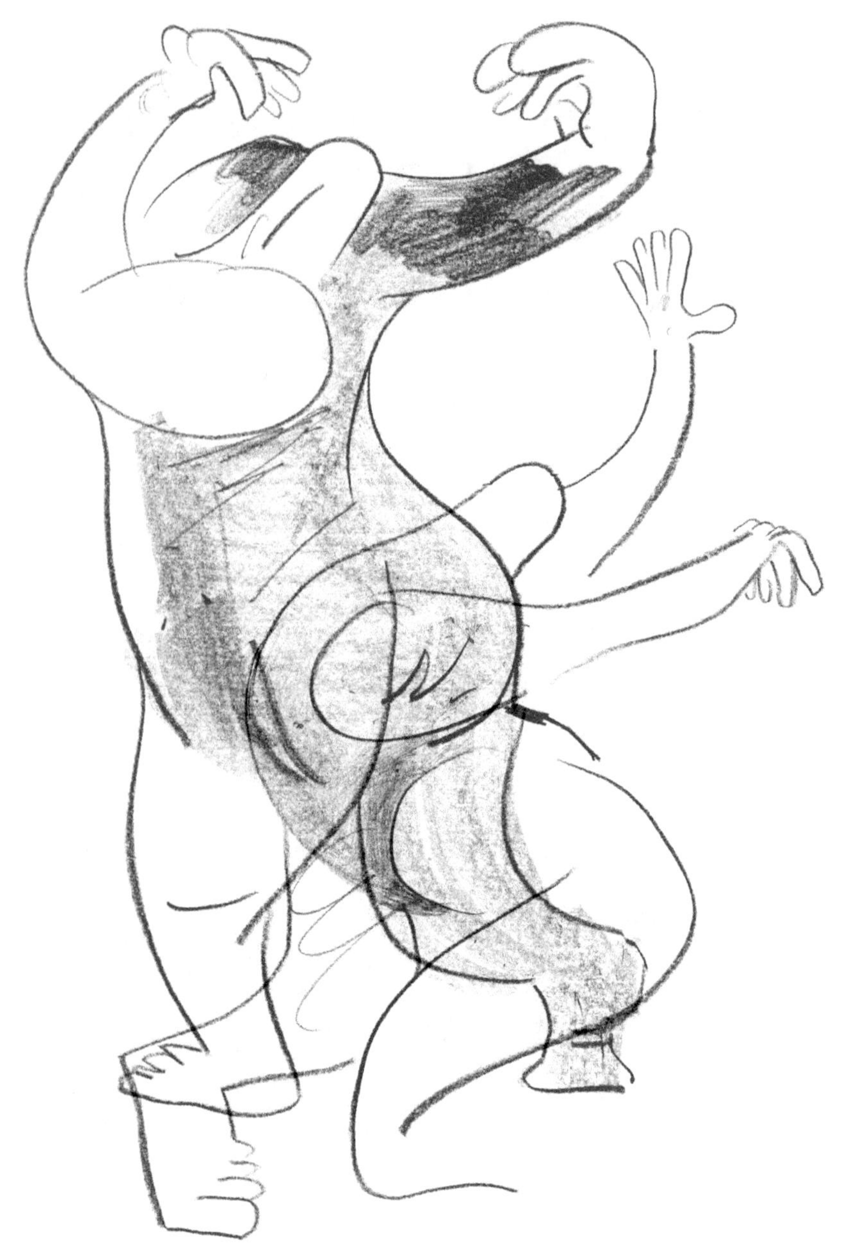

ON ANY OTHER NIGHT, THAT IN ITSELF WOULD HAVE
CONSUMED US — INDIGNANT ACCUSATIONS PUT FORTH
AT A BAR OR IN SOMEONE'S TINY APARTMENT AS WE
EACH WOULD HAVE PRESENTED OUR THEORY ON WHO
WAS TO BLAME. WHO WAS RESPONSIBLE FOR
CLEANING THE STAGE.

THIS WAS OUR LIVELIHOOD, AFTER ALL. IF SOMEONE GOT HURT, THEY WOULD BE OUT OF WORK FOR WEEKS. WE ALL TALKED ABOUT PREPARING FOR SUCH AN EVENTUALITY, ABOUT SAVING UP A BIT OF MONEY — BUT WE NEVER DID. OF COURSE.

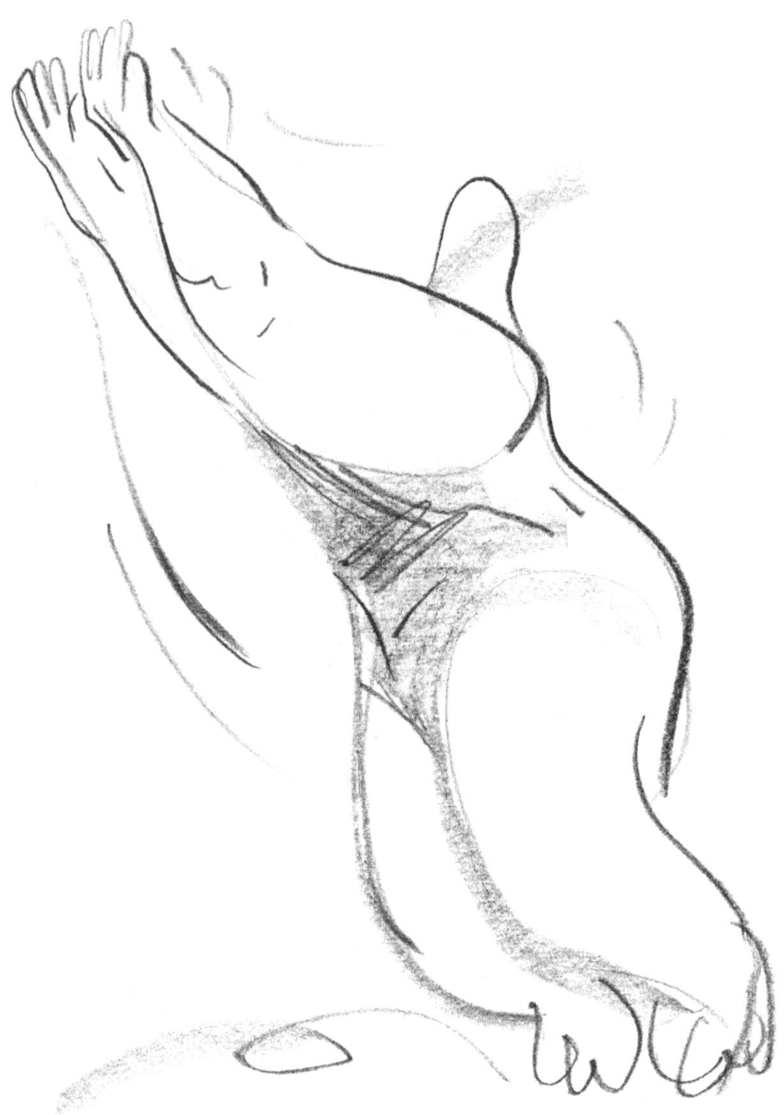

SO CLAUDIA SLIPPED AND HER ANKLE TURNED ONE WAY AND THE REST OF HER BODY TURNED THE OTHER. SHE FELL TO THE GROUND. IT HAPPENED SO FAST, WHICH EXPLAINS WHY THE QUINTESSENTIAL QUESTION WAS SO DIFFICULT TO ANSWER.

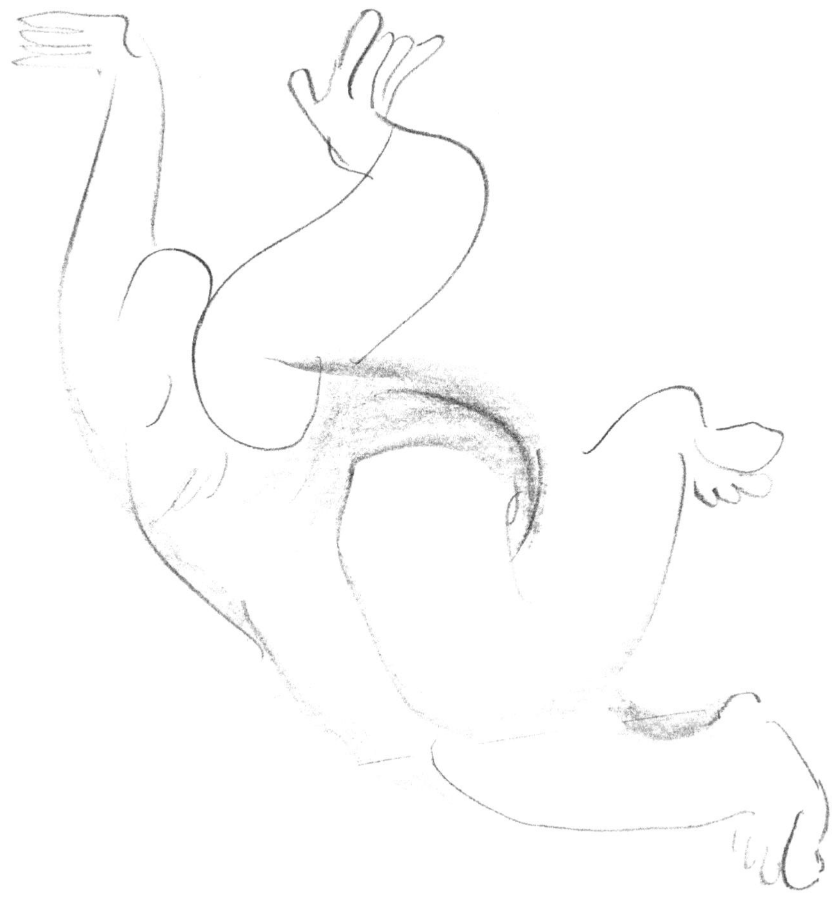

THIS IS WHAT WOULD, IN FACT, CONSUME OUR CONVERSATION FOR WEEKS TO COME: DID CLAUDIA FALL TO THE FLOOR WITH AS MUCH GRACE AND POISE AS WE ALL NOW REMEMBER? OR WAS IT VIVIAN WHO EXAGERRATED THE FLUID MOVEMENTS BURIED WITHIN A DANCER'S MOST AWKWARD STUMBLE, BRINGING THEM TO THE FORE AS SHE FELL MAJESTICALLY TO THE GROUND A FEW SECONDS AFTER CLAUDIA?

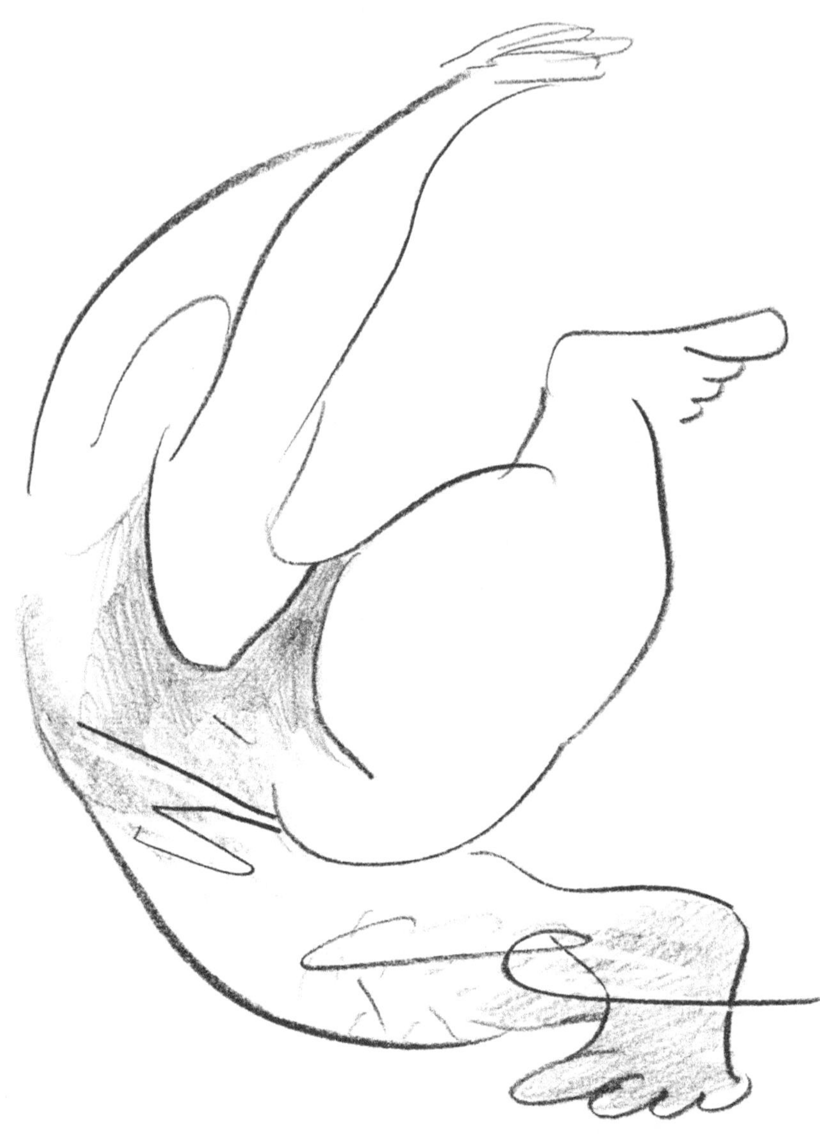

SHANNON WOULD USUALLY INTERJECT AT THIS STAGE,
ARGUING THAT AS THE THIRD DANCER TO FALL SHE
WAS THE ONE TO TRULY ESTABLISH THE RHYTHM OF
OUR IMPROVISED DISASTER. THIS POINT WAS DULY IF
ABSENTMINDEDLY NOTED AS WE EACH REPLAYED THE
KEY MOMENTS IN OUR HEAD — VIVIAN'S STUMBLE,
CLAUDIA'S SWIRL. OR VICE VERSA.

THE TWO PROTAGONISTS WERE POLITELY AGNOSTIC ON THE
MATTER, SINCERELY RECOGNIZING THE OTHER'S CONTRIBUTION
WITHOUT DIMINISHING THEIR OWN. THIS FACADE, IF THAT
IS WHAT IT WAS, REMAINED INTACT EVEN IF ONLY CLAUDIA
OR VIVIAN HAPPENED TO BE IN THE ROOM AT THE TIME.

AFTER THE SHOW, WE SHIMMERED. WE HAD, OBVIOUSLY, EACH
FALLEN TO THE GROUND IN TURN. AN INCONSEQUENTIAL
MISTAKE HAD BECOME A MOMENT OF PURE MAGIC. THERE WERE
CERTAINLY CYNICS AMONG US, BUT EVEN THEY SEEMED
TEMPORARY CONVERTS TO THE GOSPEL OF PERFORMANCE AS
MYSTICISM. IMPROVISATION AS ALCHEMY.

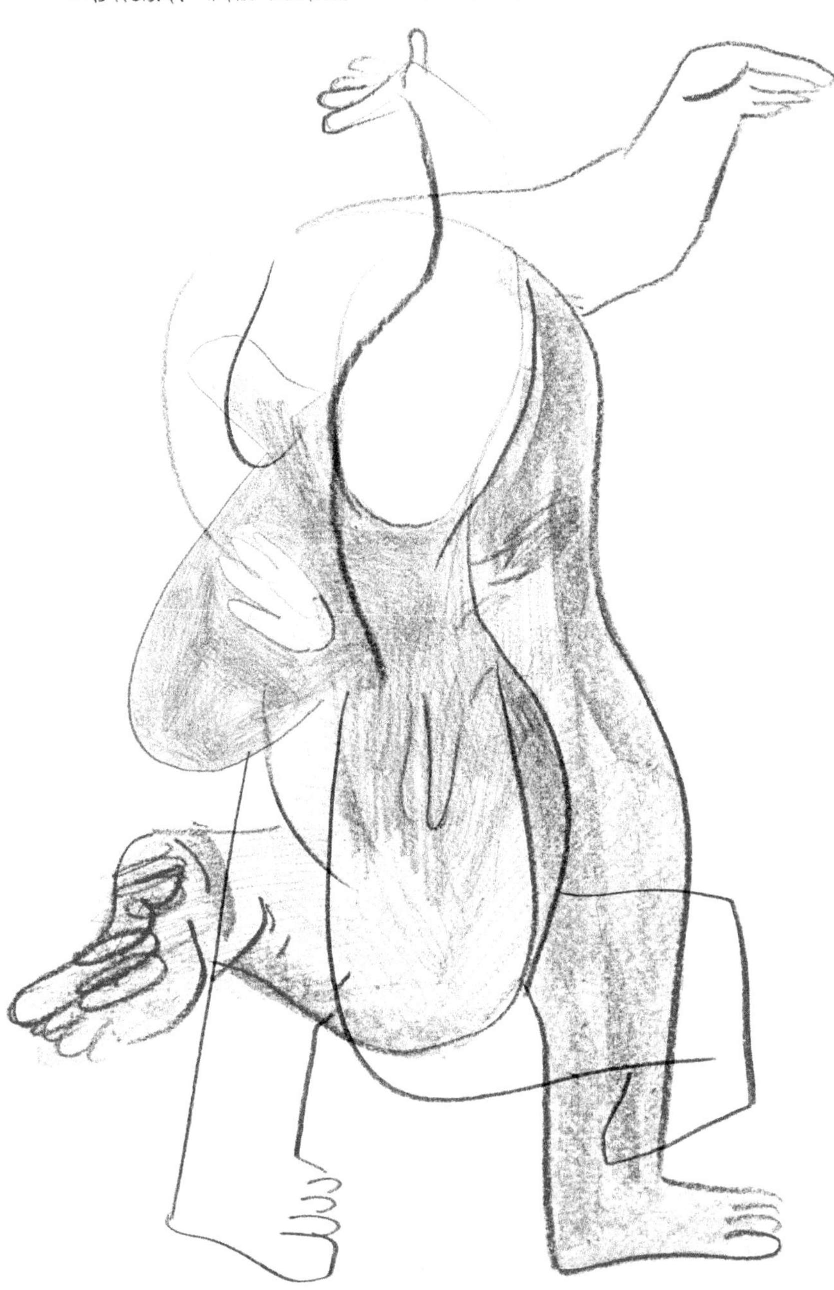

THE NEXT DAY, ANOTHER DEBATE EMERGED. WE CHECKED
IN REVIEWS, BLOG POSTS, COMMENTS FROM OUR FEW
DIEHARD FANS. AND: NOTHING. NO INDICATION, AND
CERTAINLY NO PROOF, THAT ANYTHING OUTSIDE OF THE
ORDINARY HAD OCCURED. NO MENTION OF THE FALL.

FOR SOME, THE PREVIOUS NIGHT'S SHELL OF CONFIDENCE
PROVED BRITTLE AND SOON COLLAPSED. THEY BEGAN TO
INSIST WE WERE IMAGINING THINGS, THAT THE FALL
WAS NOWHERE NEAR AS GRACEFUL OR AS IMPORTANT
AS WE HAD ASSUMED. OTHERS SCOFFED AT THE
NOTION THAT ANYONE COULD QUESTION A MOMENT
THEY THEMSELVES KNEW TO BE GOOD AND TRUE.

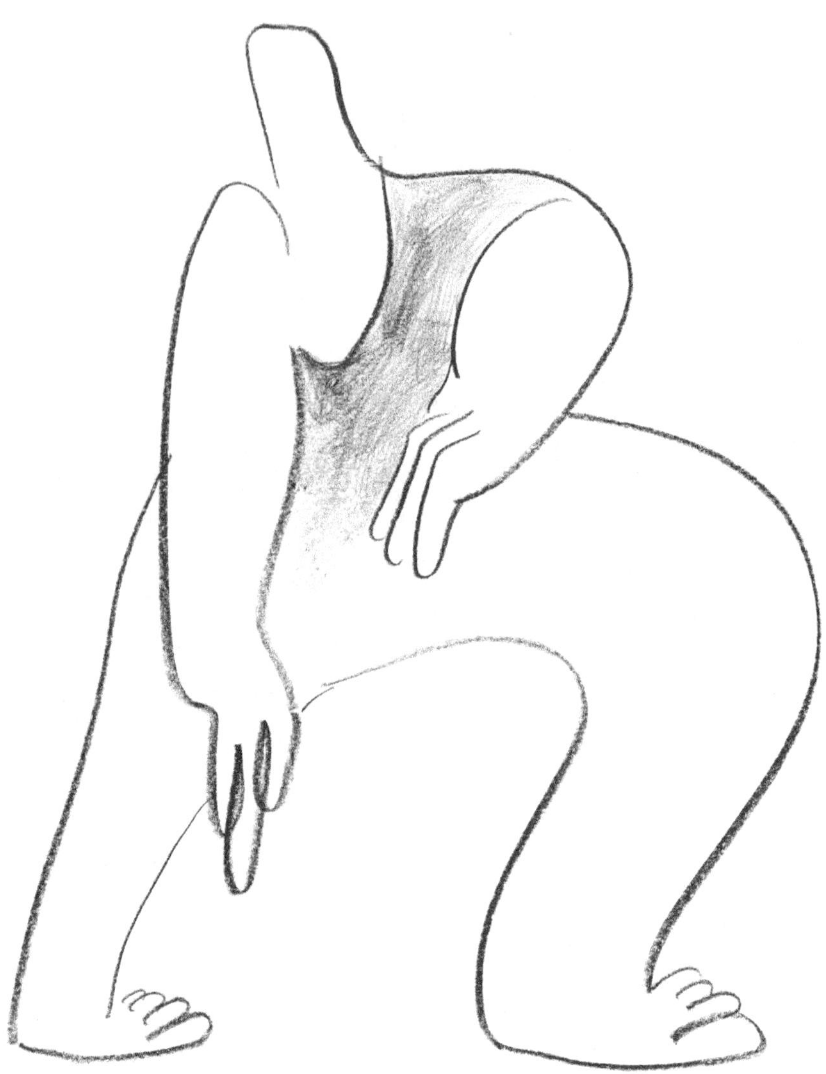

CLAUDIA WAS OUT FOR THREE WEEKS WITH A BADLY
SPRAINED ANKLE. SHE REALLY HAD FALLEN,
EVEN IF THE FALL WAS PERHAPS IMBUED WITH GRACE.
STILL, WE DID TALK ABOUT DOING THE FALL
AGAIN, MAYBE EVEN MAKING IT A PERMANENT PART
OF THE SHOW. BUT OUR PRODUCERS BALKED AT
THE PROSPECT OF ACTIVELY COURTING INJURY
EACH NIGHT.

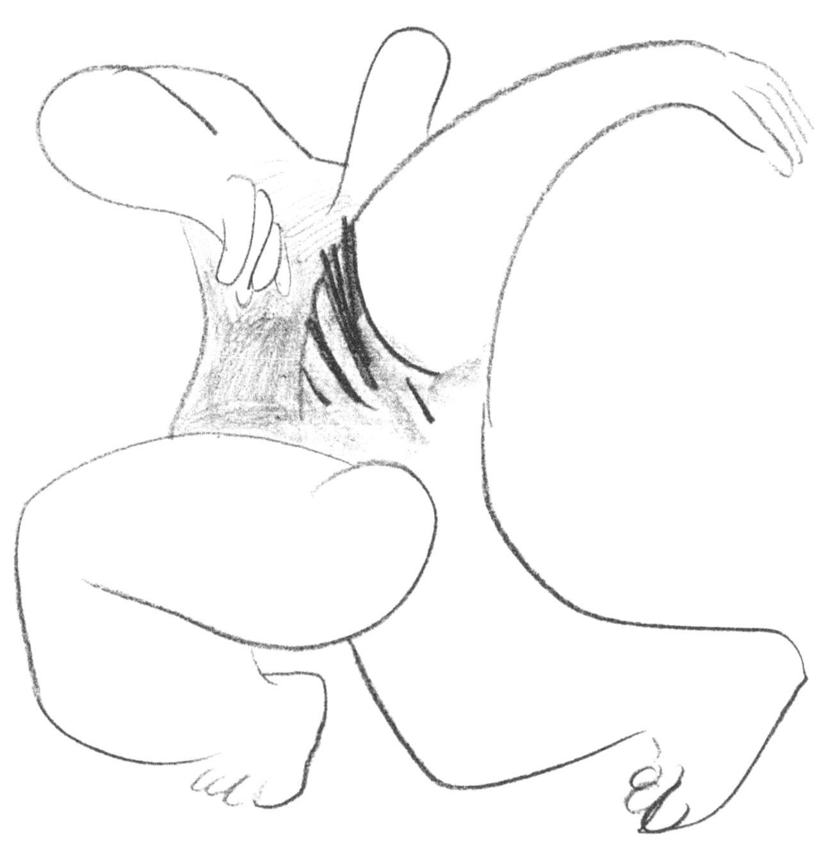

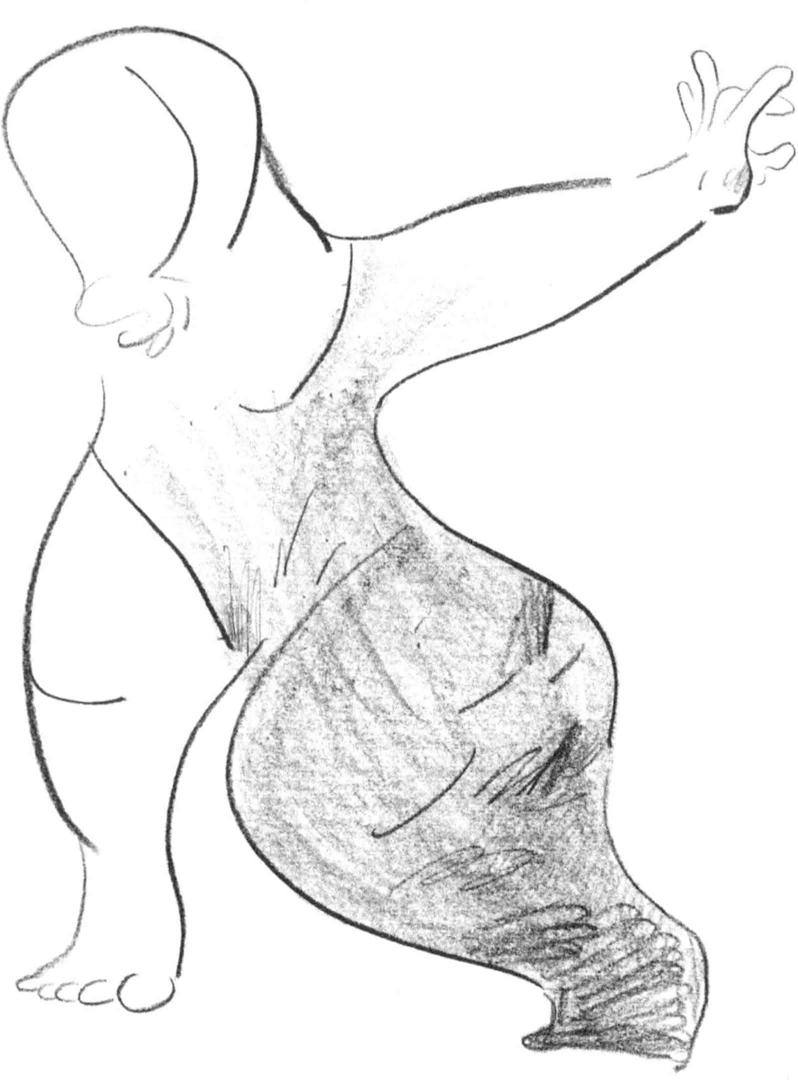

IN HINDSIGHT THEY WERE RIGHT. NONE OF US
COULD AFFORD TO GET HURT.

# SPOTTED

THE BROWN DOG LUNGED AT THE SPOTTED DOG AND STARTED BARKING, BECAUSE THAT IS WHAT DOGS SOMETIMES DO. SUDDENLY, THE OWNER OF THE SPOTTED DOG — CALL HER THE SPOTTED LADY — THREW HERSELF ON THE GROUND, WAILING AS SHE HIT THE PAVEMENT.

MAYBE SHE WAS TRYING TO PROTECT THE SPOTTED DOG, BUT SHE DID IT IN AN ESPECIALLY STUPID WAY. HER FACE WAS INCHES FROM THE BROWN DOG'S SNARLING LIPS. HE COULD HAVE BITTEN HER.

THIS IS NOT TO SAY THAT THE BROWN DOG IS A BAD DOG. I KNOW THE BROWN DOG, I HAVE PET THE BROWN DOG, AND AT TIMES I HAVE SEEN THE BROWN DOG DISPLAY HINTS OF TRUE NOBLENESS. THE BROWN DOG IS NOT A BAD DOG.

STILL, SOMETIMES BASE URGES OVERTAKE THE BEST OF US. THE SPOTTED LADY COULD EASILY HAVE BEEN BITTEN.

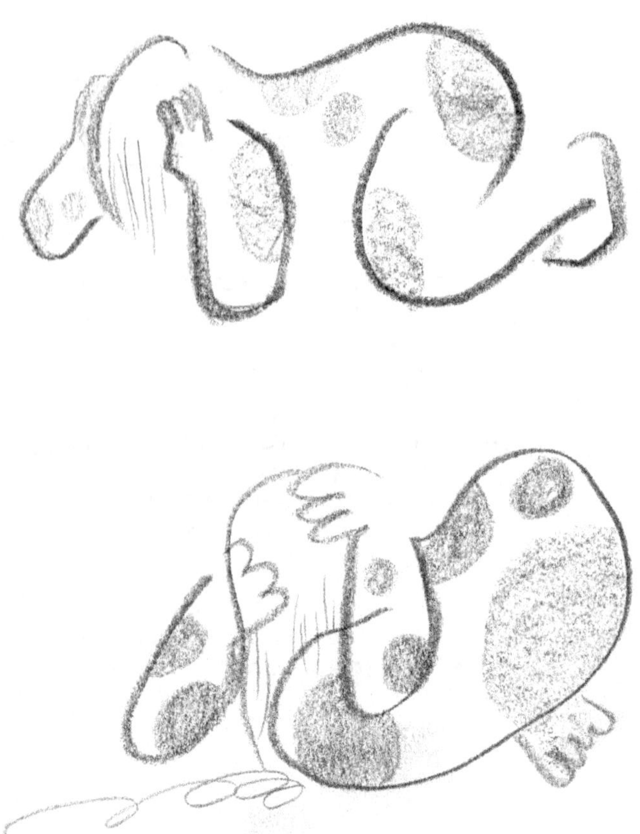

SO, ILL-ADVISED OR OTHERWISE, THE SPOTTED
LADY WAS ON THE GROUND, CONTINUING TO WAIL.
IT WAS A VAGUE, GUTTERAL SOUND. THE BROWN
DOG WAS YANKED BACK, BUT HIS OWNER'S
APOLOGIES WERE INAUDIBLE OVER
THE SPOTTED WAILS.


A CROWD HAD FORMED, AND PEOPLE NATURALLY
ASSUMED THE SPOTTED WOMAN WAS HURT. BUT BY
VIGOROUSLY SHAKING HER HEAD AND BY SHIFTING
THE WAIL TOWARDS A DESPERATE SOB, THE
SPOTTED WOMAN MANAGED TO DISPEL THEM ALL.

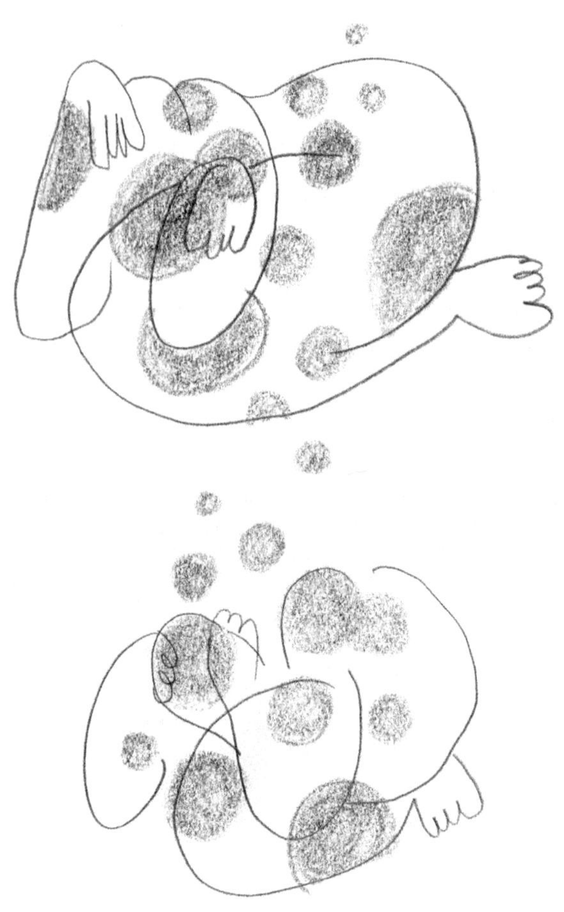

BY EVENING, WORD HAD SPREAD AND PASSERS-BY NO LONGER STOPPED TO CHECK ON HER. THE SPOTTED DOG, IT SHOULD BE SAID, SEEMED AS BEWILDERED AS THE REST OF US. IT JUST SAT THERE.

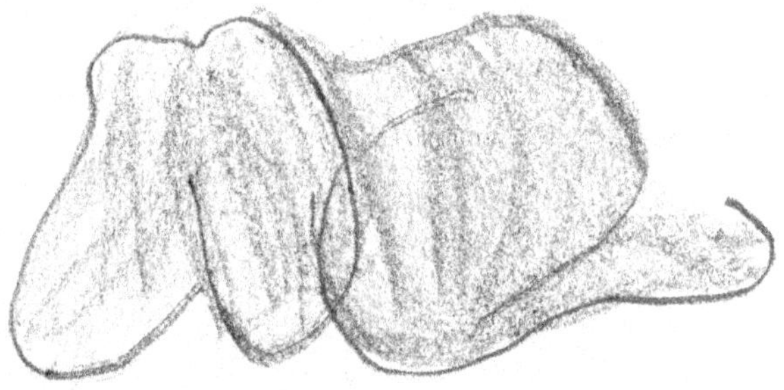

EVENTUALLY SHE WAS REMOVED, OF COURSE.
PRESUMABLY BY FORCE. BUT FOR SOME REASON
THAT TOOK SEVERAL WEEKS. AT SOME POINT
THE SPOTTED DOG DISAPPEARED, BUT FOR
THAT BRIEF PERIOD THE SPOTTED LADY
BECAME AS MUCH A PART OF THE LANDSCAPE
AS THE TREES, THE HOUSES, THE SIDEWALK.

JUST AMBIENT NOISE. VISUAL TEXTURE.

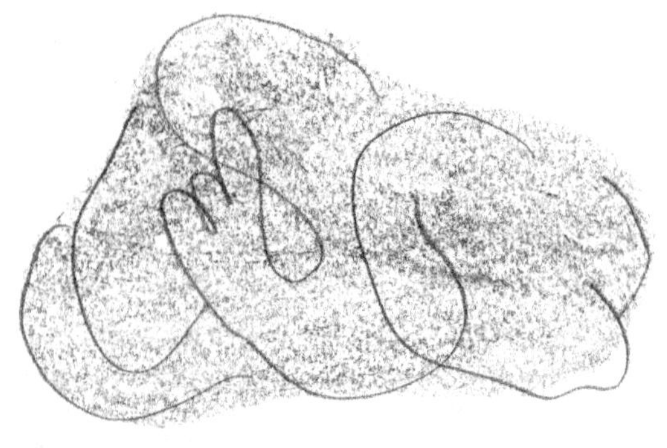

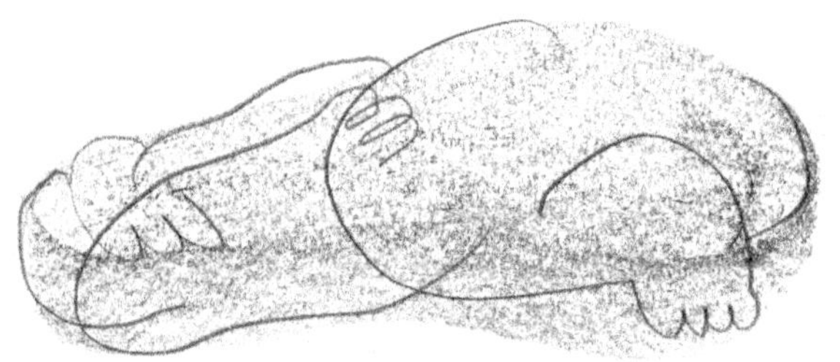

I LOOKED AT THEM

THEY WALKED
THROUGH THE
DOOR TOGETHER,
HOLDING HANDS.
A PARENT
AND A CHILD,
I THINK.
OR
AS I
LOOKED
CLOSER
IT SEEMED MORE LIKE
THEIR HANDS WERE... FUSED.
?

THEIR FACES WERE BLANK AND THEIR HANDS WERE FUSED.
AND GETTING MORE AND MORE ENTERTWINED IN FACT
I WATCHED THEM
CAREFULLY

CAREFULLY, BECAUSE I WANTED TO DISCERN IN THOSE FACES, THOSE HANDS
SOME RAY, SOME LOOSE HANGNAIL OF EMOTION
WELL, AND I WONDERED IF THEIR PALMS FELT SWEATY.

THEY STOOD THERE WITHOUT THE FEAR THAT THE REST OF US FELT.
WITHOUT THE TREPIDATION

# PIPES

A FEW WEEKS BEFORE WE ALL STOPPED LEAVING OUR HOMES, OUR ROOF STARTED TICKING.

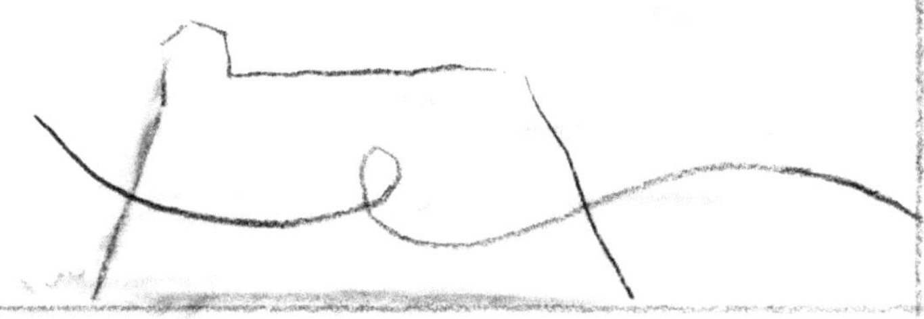

SOME KIND OF METAL EXPANDING, WE DECIDED, AS WINTER MOVED INTO SPRING AND THE DAYS GOT WARMER. IT WOULD STOP SOON ENOUGH.

BUT IT DIDN'T STOP

AND SOON WE
WEREN'T SLEEPING

IT WAS LIKE A KNIFE STABBING INTO OUR EARDRUMS.
IRREGULAR, BUT SHARP. SUDDEN. UNDENIABLE.



IT WAS LIKE A KNIFE STABBING INTO OUR EARDRUMS.
IRREGULAR, BUT SHARP. SUDDEN. UNDENIABLE.

WE STARED AT EACH OTHER AND WE STARED AT
SCREENS AND WE STARED AT THE DARKNESS AS
WE CONTINUED NOT TO SLEEP.

THE WORLD FELT LIKE IT
WAS FALLING APART AND
WE WERE VERY LUCKY
BUT SOMETIMES IT WAS
HARD TO FEEL LUCKY
THROUGH A HAZE OF
FATIGUE AND WORRY.

MAYBE THE PIPES WERE CREAKING
BECAUSE THE WALLS WERE CLOSING
IN ON US.

WE'D TRIED EARPLUGS AND WE'D TRIED
WHITE NOISE BUT HAD WE TRIED
REMEASURING THE WALLS?

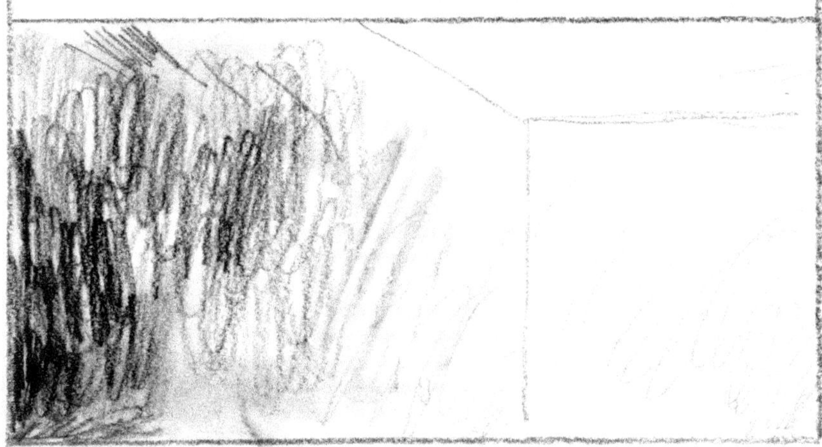

BY LATE APRIL, THE TICKING HAD GOTTEN
BETTER. AT LEAST WE CONVINCED
OURSELVES IT HAD.

BUT IT HAD ALSO MIGRATED OUT OF
THE DARKNESS AND INFECTED OUR
DAYS. IT BECAME IMPOSSIBLE NOT
TO THINK ABOUT.

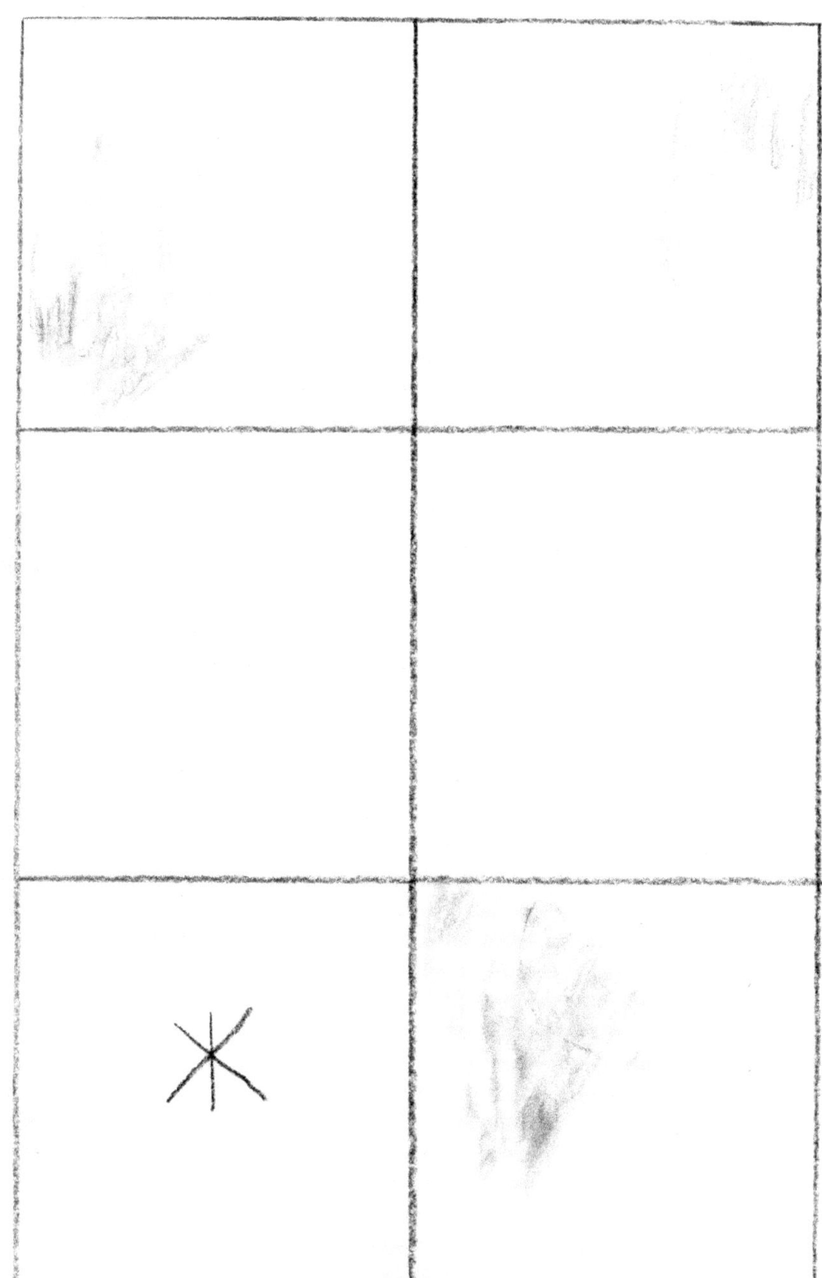

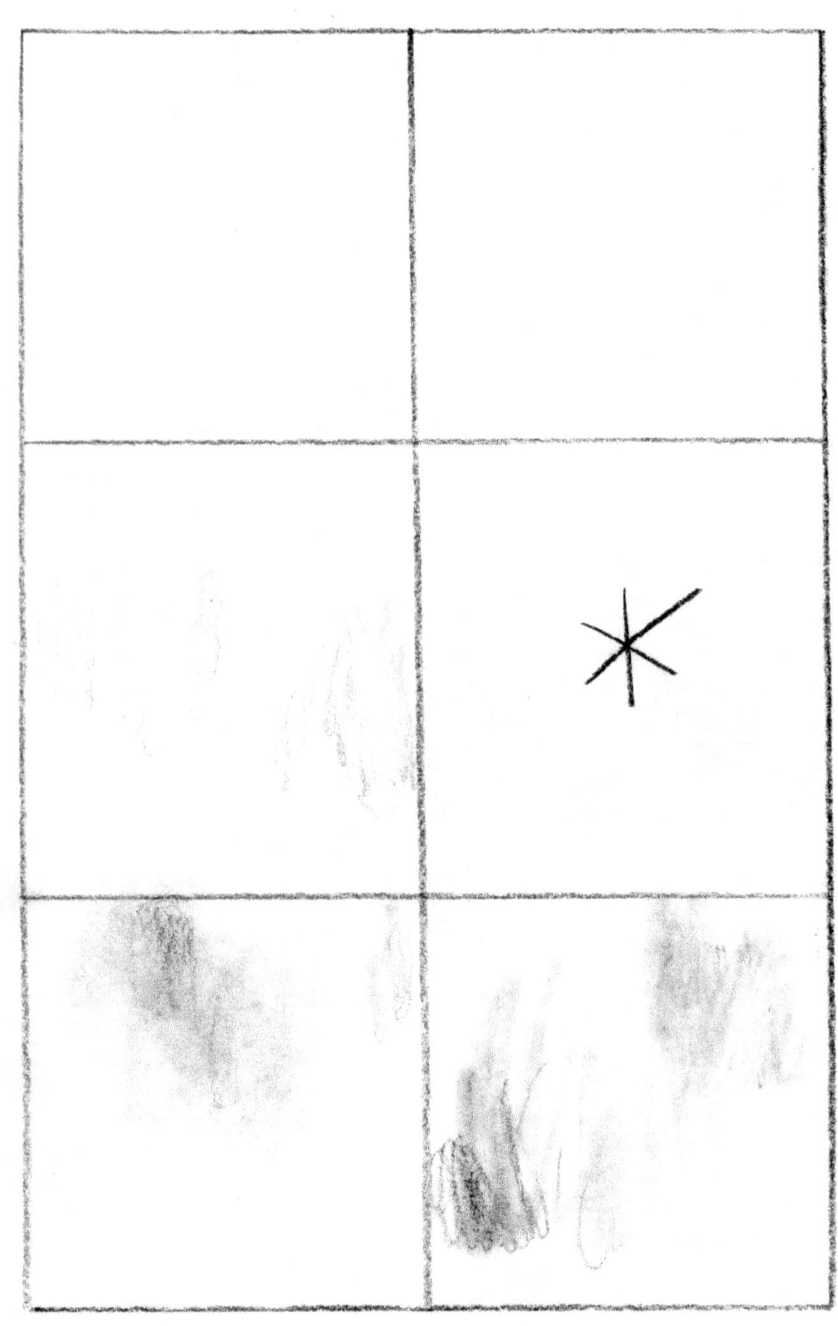

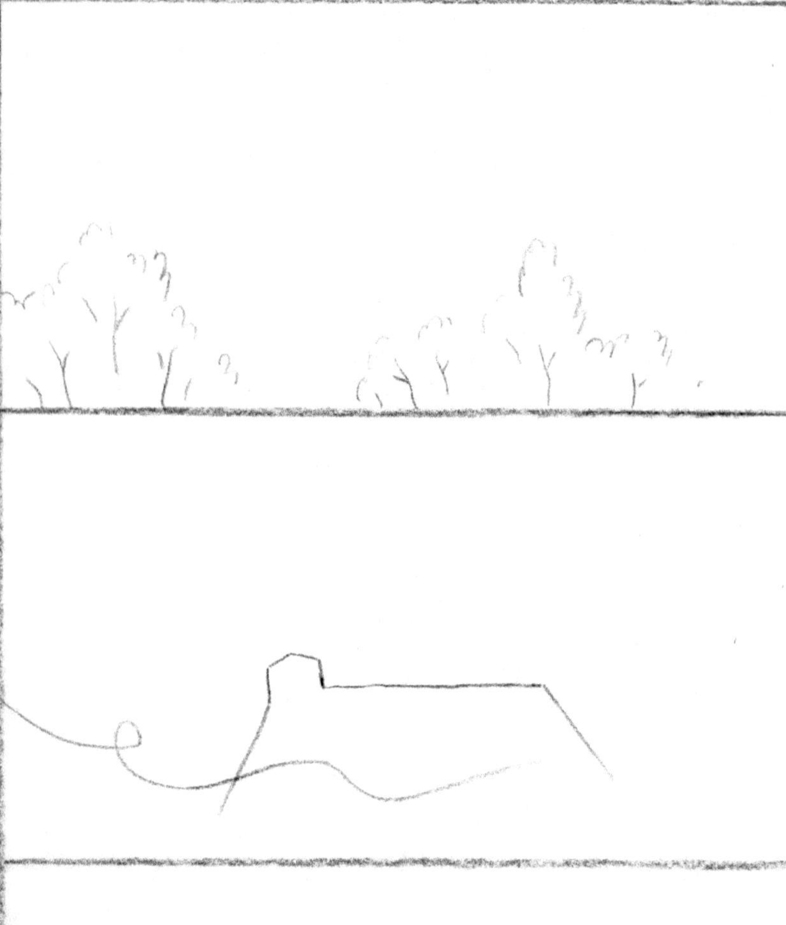

IT'S MAY. THE TICKS HAVEN'T STOPPED
BUT THEY'RE OCCASIONAL AND EASY
TO IGNORE. WE'RE SLEEPING
AGAIN, MOSTLY.

THE ONLY THING THAT KEEPS ME AWAKE THESE DAYS IS THE ENDLESS CHURN OF MY OWN ANXIETY
MAY 2020

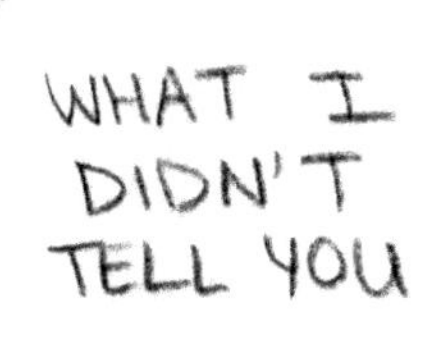
WHAT I
DIDN'T
TELL YOU

I BREATHE OUT CAREFULLY
AND I HOLD MY WORDS IN PLACE

I BREATHE OUT CAREFULLY

AND I HOLD MY WORDS IN PLACE

AND THEN I'M BACK INSIDE
BUT MY WORDS ARE STILL OUT THERE
AND THEY'LL STILL BE THERE IN THE MORNING, EVEN IF I CAN'T SEE THEM.

I SEE SOME OTHER WORDS AS I'M WALKING HOME
NORMALLY I'D STEP AROUND THEM, BUT IT'S LATE AND I'M GETTING TIRED
SO

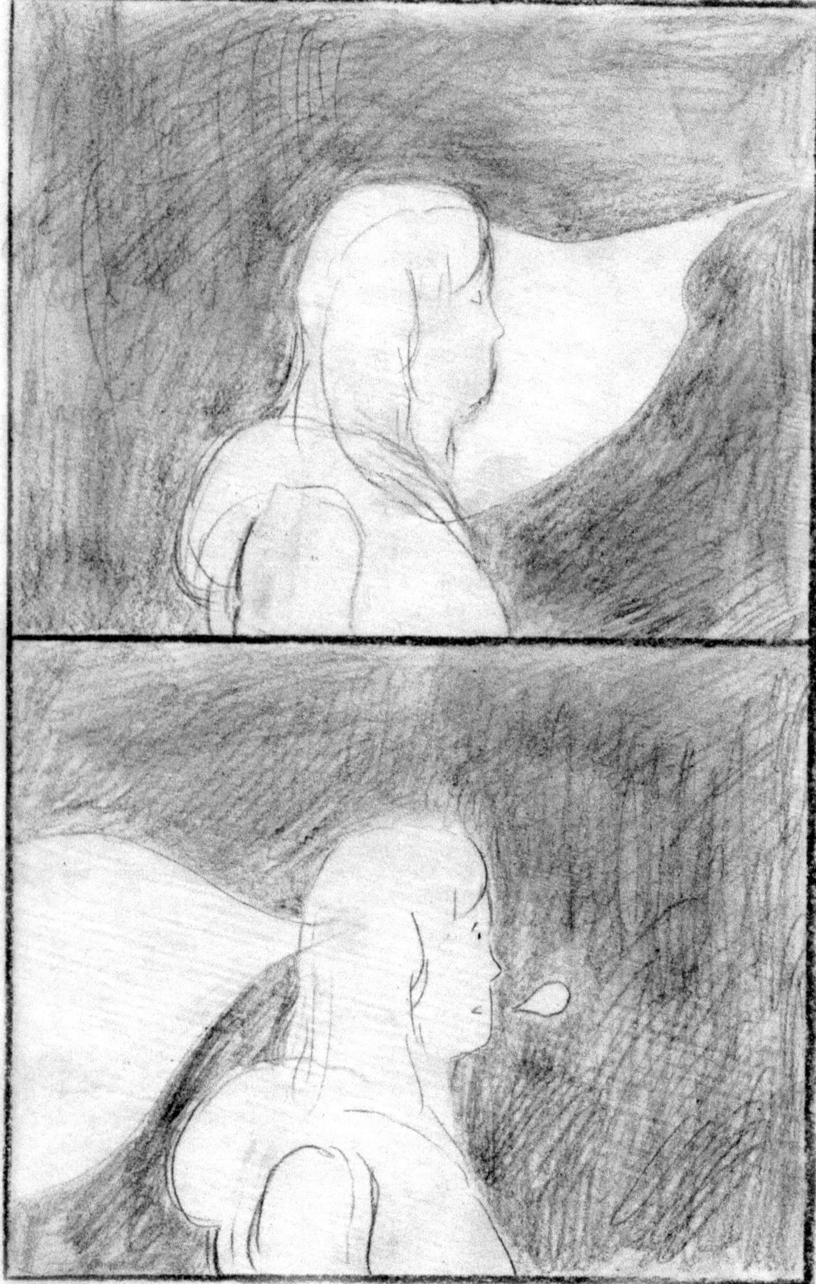

A WARM
THOUGH
THAT

FROM THEN ON, I BEGAN TEACHING MYSELF TO SWALLOW WORDS.

OR IF I CAN'T GET THEM DOWN

I HOLD THE WORDS IN MY MOUTH

THEN LET THEM COME OUT AGAIN

I
C O U GH
OUT
P O S
B
L T I E S

I'M COATED IN WHISPERS
AND I EAT SECRETS UNTIL I FEEL SICK

THEY BURN HOLES INSIDE ME
BUT FOR SOME REASON I CAN'T STOP
MAY 2020

(minutes)

i'm
watching
for
movement

i want to squeeze
the air out of
the middle distance

will the trees
grow longer
before my heart
stops shaking?

i see whispers of motion
i enjoy the lie of stillness
i try to
watch
the sun

break
up
time
(i climb the
seconds brick
by brick)

i count leaves
i trace outlines

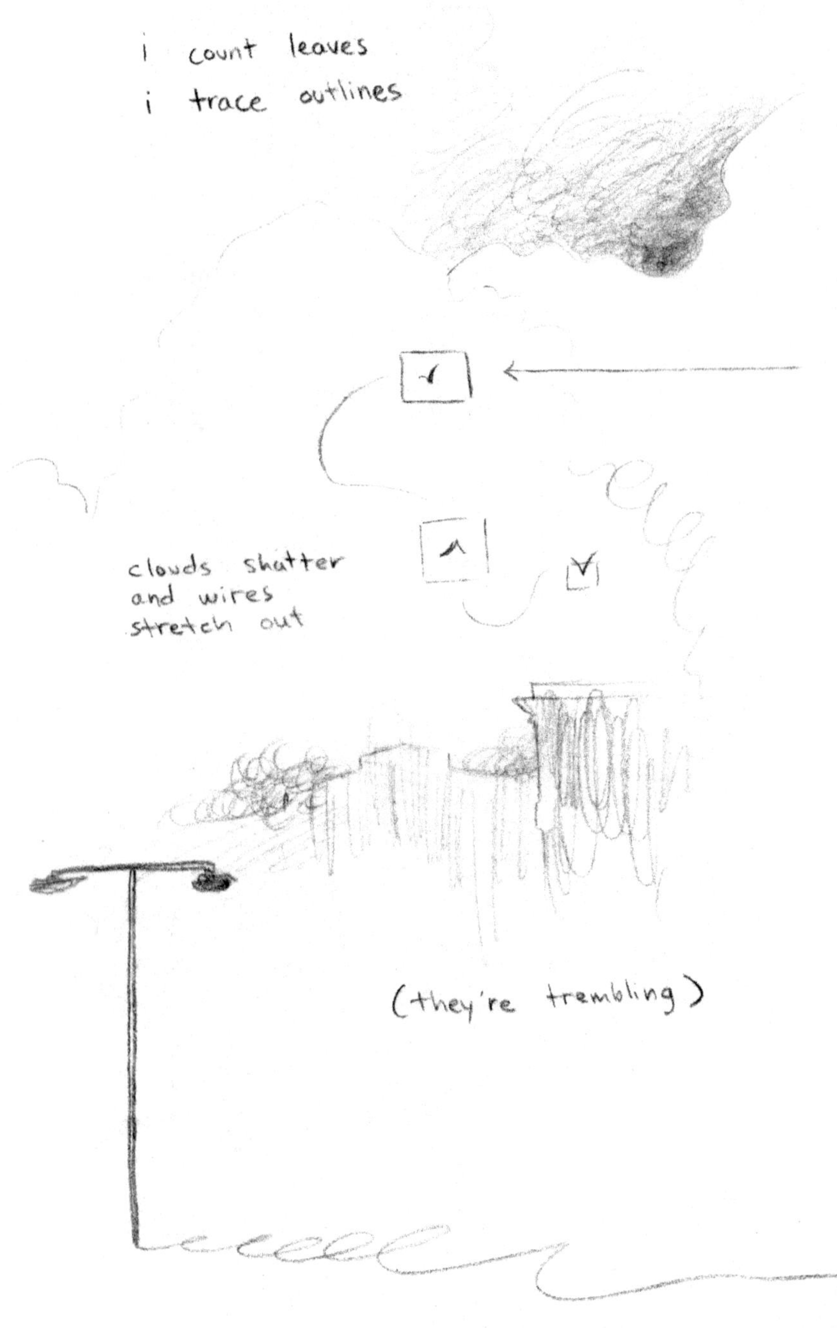

my eyelids shudder
and i hope the shadows
might warn me of what
is to come
MAY- 20
JUN 20

# SADNESS

I WONDER SOMETIMES —
WHAT IS THE SHAPE
OF SADNESS?

AND IF I KNEW, COULD
I HOLD THAT SHAPE
IN MY HAND?

IF I HELD SADNESS
IN MY HANDS,
HOW MIGHT IT FEEL?

SADNESS IS A BLACK SLUDGE THAT SEEPS OUT OF US AND
COVERS THE FLOOR. WE STUMBLE TOWARDS HOPE, PERHAPS,
BUT WE'RE MOVING SO SLOWLY. OUR LEGS ARE TIRED.

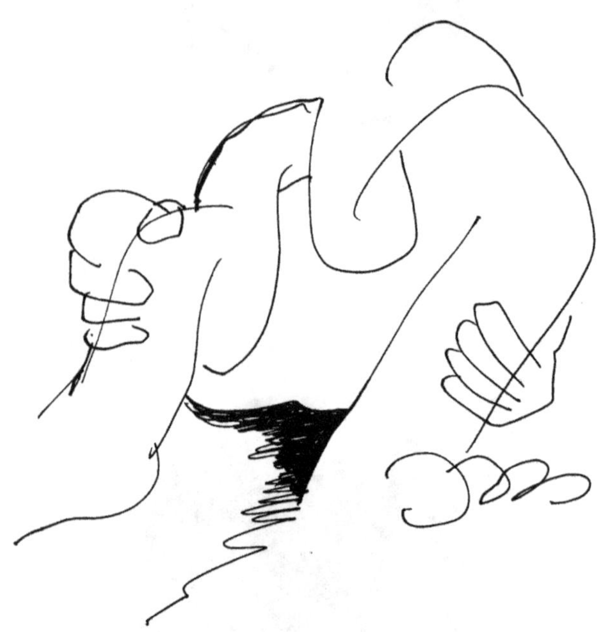

WOULDN'T IT BE BETTER TO SLEEP?

WE SAY THAT WE STARE INTO THE MIDDLE DISTANCE.
DOES THIS MEAN THAT NEARER TO US IS NOW AND
FARTHER FROM US IS TOMORROW AND WE WANT TO BURY
OURSELVES BETWEEN THE SECONDS?

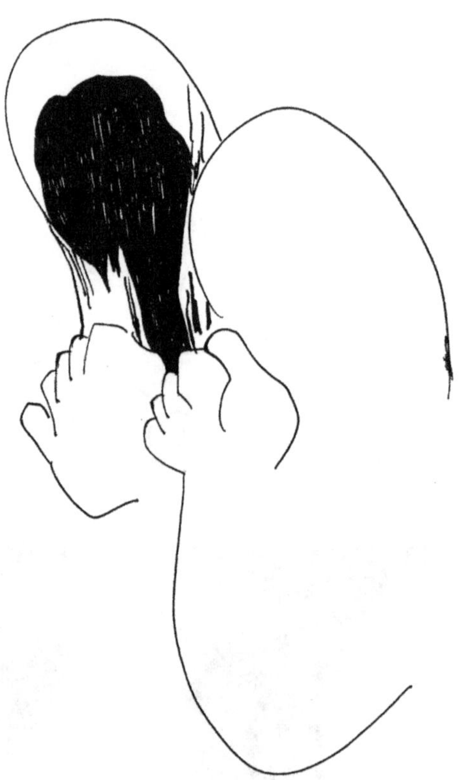

BECAUSE SOMETIMES SADNESS
MEANS HOPING TIME WILL
PASS US BY.

WE SINK DOWN INTO OURSELVES.

WE'RE FALLING BUT
WE'RE NOT MOVING.

THE AIR CLOSES IN,
SQUEEZING THE BUOYANCY
OUT OF OUR LIVES.

AND WE BEGIN
TO DREAD TOMORROW.

# "TOMORROW"

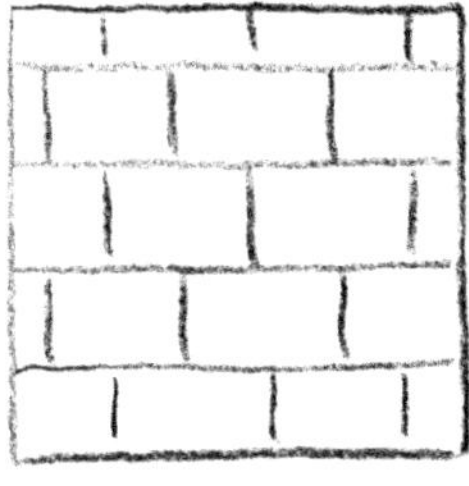

ONCE THEY HAD REMOVED ONE BRICK, THE REST WAS EASY.

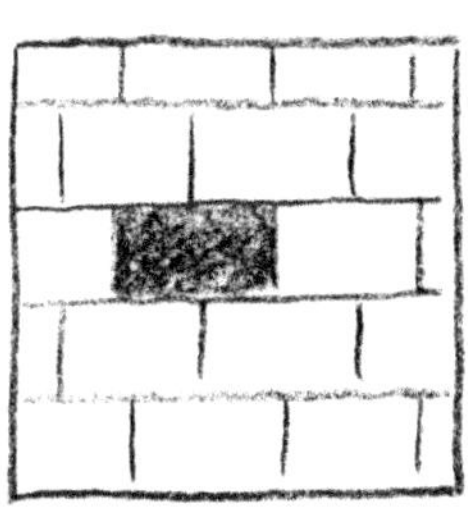

THERE WAS FIRE IN THEIR STOMACHS AND HOPE IN THEIR HEARTS SO THEY MOVED QUICKLY.

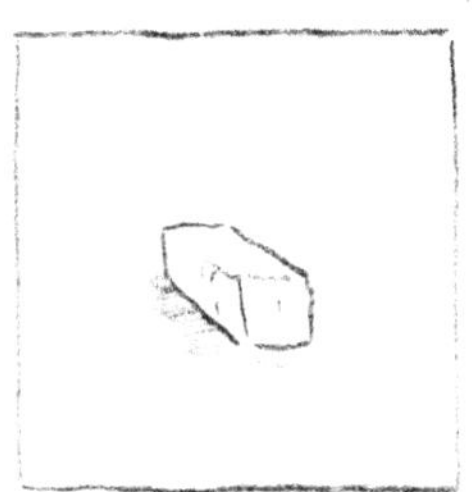

NERVES SHOOK, WAVES CRASHED. DECADES PASSED.

THEIR SKIN WAS DRY AND FADING.

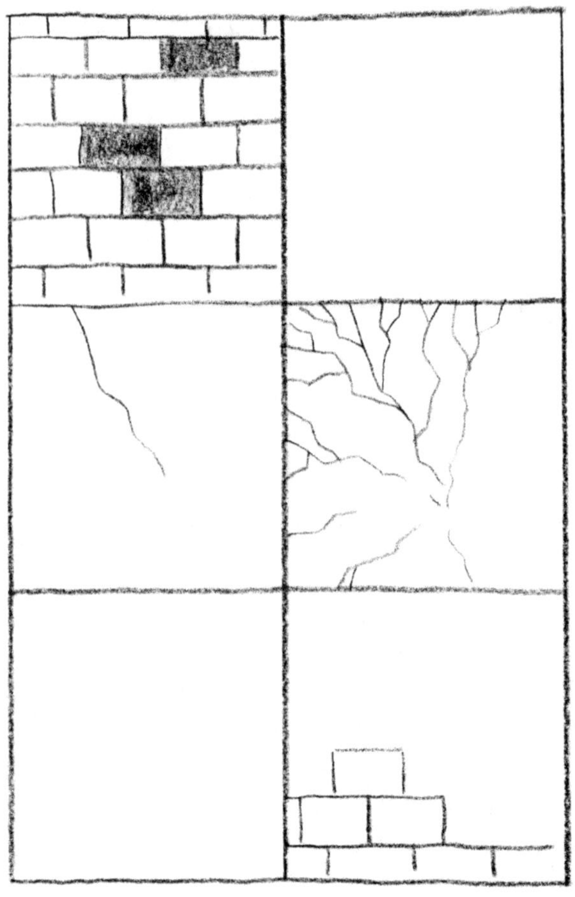

AND THEN THEY WERE DONE
THE WALL WAS STILL THERE,
BUT AT LEAST NOW
IT WAS INVISIBLE

THAT WAS SOMETHING.

THE WIND WAS AT THEIR BACKS,
SOFTLY BLOWING, SO ALTHOUGH
THEY WERE VERY TIRED
THEY FELT GOOD.

THEY LOOKED THROUGH THE WALL.

WHEN THEY WERE DONE, THEY
PICKED UP THE BRICKS

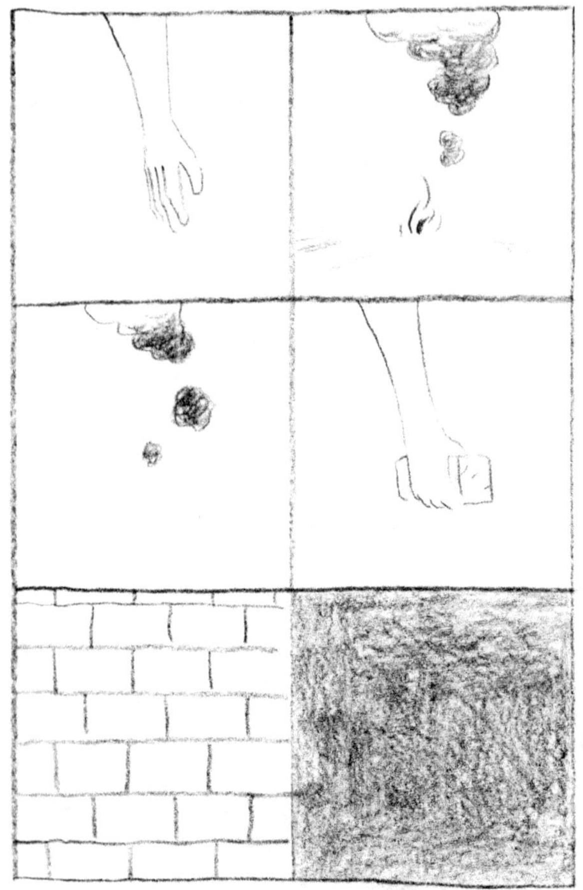

AND THEY WENT TO BUILD
SOMETHING NEW.

www.ingramcontent.com/pod-product-compliance
Lightning Source LLC
Chambersburg PA
CBHW070654100726
47907CB00007B/2198